JESSIE HAAS

Westminster West

Greenwillow Books, New York

Printed in the United States of America
First Edition   10 9 8 7 6 5 4 3 2

Library of Congress Cataloging-in-Publication Data

Haas, Jessie.
    Westminster West / by Jessie Haas.
        p.   cm.
    Summary: Two sisters struggle with their roles as women
within the family and within society as an arsonist
threatens their post–Civil War Vermont community.
    ISBN 0-688-14883-2
    [1. Sisters—Fiction.   2. Sex role—Fiction.
3. Farm life—Fiction.
4. Vermont—History—1865—Fiction.
5. Arson—Fiction.]   I. Title.
PZ7.H1129We   1997   [Fic]—dc20
96-7096   CIP   AC

For my father,
Robert J. Haas,
and
for my sister,
Martha

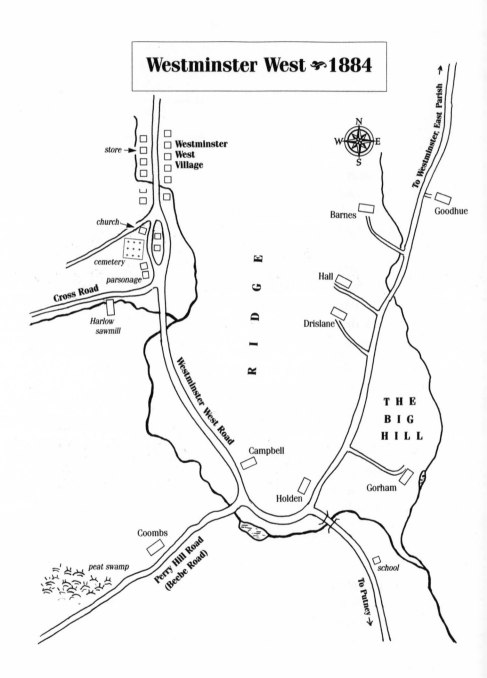

Westminster West ❧ 1884

store → Westminster West Village

N
W E
S

To Westminster, East Parish →

Barnes

Goodhue

church →

cemetery

parsonage

Hall

Cross Road

Drislane

Harlow
sawmill

R I D G E

Westminster West Road

THE
BIG
HILL

Campbell

Holden

Gorham

Coombs

peat swamp

Perry Hill Road
(Beebe Road)

school

To Putney →

Prologue

Westminster lies in the northeastern part of the
county . . . bounded north by Rockingham, east by the
west bank of the Connecticut River, south by Putney,
and west by Brookline and Athens. . . . The surface of
the town is . . . quite rough and mountainous, though
there are large tracts of level land with arable
soil. . . . This brokenness of surface, though it in many
places precludes profitable cultivation, greatly
enhances the picturesqueness of the scenery, which is
proverbial for its beauty.

> Gazetteer & Business Directory of Windham
> County, Vermont, 1724–1884, compiled and
> published by Hamilton Child

Westminster West is a post village in the western part
of the town. It has one church (Congregational), a
schoolhouse, several mechanic shops, etc., and about a
dozen dwellings.

> Gazetteer, 1884

When I came here [1842] there was no railroad in the
state. . . . A telegraph was not known, a telephone was
a thing unheard of. These means of communication have
connected larger towns, but left this parish out in the

cold. *We must go out to get into the current that is rushing by. Few come in.*

Rather than feel that our parish is small, let us look upon it as large enough for our best efforts. . . . As an inducement to faithfulness in the field given for us to cultivate . . . remember, our time is passing rapidly. Looking back from the point we occupy today, I do not see anything that has stood still. As I look back, I see the youth and children of the parish that met me 40 years ago, rushing by me, some out into the broad fields of active life. They are soon lost to sight. Some to the grave. The passer-by reads today the date of their birth and death. That is all that is known of them. I see, too, those that were then the occupants of these farms, passing by me. The sound of their driving, their threshing, their buying and selling soon ceases. The grave holds silent watch over them to-day. I see those of the parish then approaching manhood, rushing by me, to take the places their fathers had just left, striking out for larger fields and with a rush grasping for more than their fathers had, and in a few years of struggle lie down in the grave, or they are lost to my sight in the great business thoroughfares of our growing country. I see, too, the aged of the parish that met me then, moving by me with halting steps. They are soon out of my sight. Their sun quickly goes down before me. It is as still as night where they were. It seems but the work of the day passing in my dreams at night. No, nothing stands still here that is of lasting interest to me or you or the world. It is the great interest of humanity that crowds upon our thoughts and pushes us to the front and onward, and urges us to faithfulness for the Master who has given us this vineyard to cultivate. This vineyard. Here in this narrow valley we find our field of labor. Here we measure our strength for usefulness, and count the results of our lives that are to appear at the judgment day.

Alfred Stevens, D.D., February 22, 1883, address on the fortieth anniversary of his pastorate with the Congregational Church, Westminster West

1

If it had not been so very warm that day, Sue thought later.

If Clare had not been feeling delicate.

If Clare had not been encouraged to consider herself delicate, and if she had not used this as a ladylike weapon against Sue, who was not thought delicate.

If none of those novels with wasting heroines had been written, or if Mother had not allowed them to be read.

If it had not been time to cultivate the corn. If Ed or Henry had been there, to stand in the attic and take the bolts and bundles of fabric as they were passed through the trapdoor.

Even, if the South had not kept slaves, or the North not hated slavery. If Sumter had not been fired on. If Father and Otis Buxton, Walter Ranney, and Tolman Coombs had not gone away to war, or if, almost twenty years ago now, they had not come back as they did.

It was a long string of ifs. Later, when Sue came to add them up, there seemed many points at which it all might have been changed, where everything might have come out differently.

But as she thought longer, she realized that all these ifs were too large to change. The world had been setting them up to happen for a long, long time, and they *would* happen. They had to happen. Even the very smallest. Even the sticky summer morning when the fabric was laid away in the attic.

"Is that the last?" Sue asked, bending to the trapdoor. Her nose prickled with dust, and strands of hair stuck to her forehead.

Mother held up the package of muslin scraps. A trickle of sweat rolled down her brow. "Yes. Make sure you lay southernwood between all the folds, Sue, and close the latches tight. Clare, why don't you go and rest? You're looking pale."

Typical! Sue thought, straightening abruptly. *She* was roasting up here in the attic, *Mother* was toiling up and down stairs with muslin, calico, lawn, and jersey—and *Clare*, who was getting the new dresses and going on the vacation, was the one for whom it was all too much!

She shoved the muslin into the trunk, slammed the lid, and struggled with the stiff latch. Unexpectedly the hasp slid into place and pinched her finger.

"*Ow!*" Sue put her finger in her mouth and tasted blood. At the same moment she saw the dusty green southernwood branches on the floor beside the chest.

"*Confound* it!" She reached for the southernwood, and a drop of blood, dark red like a ripe cherry, fell to the floor. Another and another: big round drops, beading on the dusty board.

Sue stared at them for a moment. Then she twisted her handkerchief around her finger, lifted the lid, and thrust the sharp-smelling herb branches into the folds of muslin. Slam! went the lid, snap! went the latch, and Sue hunched on the big curved lid, gripping her finger tightly. What if she just stayed here? Would Mother worry? Would she realize that Sue, too, might be affected by the heat, might possibly have fainted up here in the sweltering attic?

Of course not! Sue was the sturdy daughter, the one who could be counted on. She turned on the trunk lid, staring into the blackest corner of the eaves and drawing the attic dimness over her like a blanket.

Before her was a yellowing stack of *Harper's Weekly*s from the time of the war, and beside them the trunk in which Father's worn uniform and Mother's wedding gown lay folded in symbolic embrace, as they had embraced after their long separation. That trunk also held christening gowns and children's clothes, the growth of the family from 1865, when it began, till now, 1884. Sue and Clare had spent one rainy afternoon when they were younger, arranging the clothes in order so they told the Gorham story.

Nothing told the story of what was happening now.

When she and Clare arranged things that day, they both were heroines. The pageant of events led in a direct line to themselves.

Nowadays only Clare was a heroine—delicate Clare, resting on the sofa, keeping her clothes clean and her hands soft, traipsing off on a *second* vacation with Aunt Emma Campbell.

It's not *fair!* Sue thought. It was supposed to be *my* turn! But "fair" and "turn" were not words to apply to special favors. Mother had made that very clear. "Your aunt asked Clare because she knows Clare better and is fond of her. She's under no obligation to either of you."

She might be fond of me, too, if she got to know me! Sue thought. But that was not the way things happened in their family. Clare was the frail one, who needed vacations. Henry was eldest son, promising young farmer. Ed, with his beautiful singing voice, his talent for painting, his charm and ambition, was like a comet, briefly illuminating their sky on his way out to the broader universe.

And Sue? An extra pair of hands for Mother, plain and simple.

The corner of the eaves swam. Two drops formed on her lower lids and spilled over, warm and wet. They felt good, but stare as she might, no more came, only a slight welling of moisture, which caught and spangled the slant of light from the gable window. Sue turned her head, letting the spangles slide along the sunbeam, all the way back to the dark corner where a patch of red, the color of her own blood on the attic floor, slowly came into focus.

Could there be something in this attic she'd never seen before?

She slid off the trunk and ducked under the steep slope of the roof. Her fingers brushed the red object but couldn't dislodge it. It was a book, jammed tight against the bottom of the rafter. Something, a nail or a knot, held it. Sue pried her fingers underneath, and with a scraping sound it came free. She brought it to the light. It was a small red leather book, with the fresh brown scratch she had just torn across the front cover. She blew off the dust and opened it.

The page was covered with a firm, well-formed script in brownish ink. Familiar handwriting. Probably one of Grandfather's diaries, in which he had written every day such tidings as "Rained. Picked 12 quarts strawberries. Got out 2 loads manure."

Oh, well. Father would be pleased. He turned back to the diaries often, shaking his head at the way the currants ripened on the same date year after year. Or he'd smile at some old-fashioned farming practice, finally winning the arguments Grandfather had so often won in life.

4

Sue was about to shut the book when the words at the bottom of the page caught her eye. ". . . trembled, and felt myself the Enemy."

"Sue?" Mother didn't sound worried. She sounded sharp. "Time to start dinner! Are you having trouble with the trunk?"

Sue thrust the little book into the pocket of her dress. It was not one of Grandfather's diaries, and before she showed it to anyone else, she was going to find out what it was.

"Yes, I am having trouble," she said, heading toward the trapdoor. "I cut my finger."

2

As SHE REACHED the bottom of the stairs, Sue glanced into the front parlor. Clare reclined gracefully on the sofa, with a small embroidery hoop in her hand. She set a stitch and looked up.

"Did you say something?"

"What is there to say?"

In the kitchen Mother was mixing biscuits. "Wash your finger and I'll tie it up for you."

Sue pumped cold water over her hand. Mother had a clean, soft cloth ready and tied it on in a flat knot. "Now get the potatoes going, please, and then you can shell the peas."

"Couldn't Clare shell the peas?"

"I want Clare to rest," Mother said. "We have enough to do without nursing a sick child into the bargain."

Sue hung the basket over her arm and went down the cellar stairs. It was cool, but dark, too, and in spite of weekly sweeping, there were spiders. She reached deep into the nearly empty potato bin, where the long white sprouts reached back, all wiggly . . .

"Ugh!" Sue seized a handful of sprouts and lifted the potatoes that way, counted, grabbed another batch.

Upstairs quickly; scrub the potatoes; pump water into a cooking pan, and carry the potatoes out to the stove in the summer kitchen.

Now for the peas, picked this morning and waiting in the shade beside the back door. At least shelling peas could be done sitting down—which was why it wouldn't hurt Clare to do it!

Clare used to *want* to help, Sue thought, settling on a stool with the bowl in her lap. All through her childhood Clare's hands were beside hers—smaller, weaker, but helping: pushing the churn, seizing the feather duster, shelling peas. . . . Clare saying, "Let *me!*" Clare saying, "I'll do it by myself!" It used to be annoying, Clare trying to do things she wasn't able to. It was showing off, Sue used to think, because Clare didn't like being the baby.

But when Sue was thirteen and Clare twelve Clare caught a fever, and the whole order of the house collapsed. Mother was almost always in Clare's room and, when she came out, she didn't seem to see anything outside her own thoughts. For a whole month Sue cooked, washed, cleaned. Neighbors and relatives helped with the big jobs, but the everyday work was all Sue's.

Gradually the blurry, flushed look of fever left Clare's face. Mother came out of the sickroom, and Sue waited for praise, and for the chance to tell all she'd endured. The days when she'd thought she couldn't do one single thing more, and then she did. The way she remembered Father's special stock for Sundays. The technique she'd figured out for piecrust.

But Mother just said, "Well done, Sue!" Three years later Sue was still waiting for more.

Nothing went back to the way it had been. When Clare was well enough, Aunt Emma took her to the seashore to recuperate. Clare returned a young lady. Sue was still just a big sturdy farm girl.

"Mercy, it's hot!" Mother came out with a pan of biscuit dough, opened the oven, and pushed it in. As she straight-ened, she seized the hissing teakettle and poured hot water on the slices of salt pork. Steam billowed. The last pea rattled into the pot, and Sue rushed to set them cooking.

She started the coffee, then brought the pies from the pantry—apple, mince, custard, and one last slice of rhubarb. She filled the milk pitcher. Butter, a pitcher of cool water, a plate of pickles.

As she finished, Mother came in and surveyed the table. "There! That's a morning's work!"

When the clang of the dinner bell had died away, it was quiet in the dooryard. One sleepy hen crooned to herself. Over the high, round hill to the north the Drislanes' conch shell sounded, calling their men to dinner. Over other hills, other conch shells, other bells, other men leaving the fields to eat a noontime meal.

Father and the boys unhitched from the cultivators and rode up the long, flat cornfield, Father and Henry on the big horses, Ed in the lead on the Morgan, Bright.

Bright was Sue's horse, in spirit if not in fact. She had named him when he was a new red colt stretched out on the May grass. Within three months his coat had turned nearly black, but Bright was still the right name. Even in heavy harness he looked gay and jaunty, ready for adventure.

Adventure! Sue looked up the farm road, dappled with black midday shadows. It rambled east past the sheep barn, around a little bend and up a hill to the main road. Come along! it seemed to say. Let's go somewhere!

But there was work to do, stretching through the afternoon to suppertime. Besides, Sue knew every rut and turn for as far as she could expect to travel. Every farmhouse, and every person in every house. Every horse. Every dog.

Well, I'm cross! she told herself, turning to splash her face in the basin beside the door.

Over dinner Henry continued his breakfast lecture on the feasibility of feeding corn silage to cattle.

"After all, a cow's stomach ferments fodder, doesn't it? So why should fodder that's been fermented beforehand do a cow any harm? They used to feed the pomace from cider mills to cattle, and around breweries they feed out the fermented grain—"

Ed twinkled his eyes across the table at Clare and Sue. "Fascinating, hmm?"

"At least it isn't the fires!"

"At least it isn't the fires!"

Sue felt her face go red, Clare frowned at her plate, and Ed's smile widened teasingly. "You two sound like twins!"

"What about the fires?" Henry asked.

Ed laughed. "The girls were saying they never want to hear another word about the fires. I think it was a mistake to mention it, myself."

Henry looked at them indignantly. "Three barns burned inside of two months, some kind of maniac on the loose, and you girls don't think it's worth talking about?"

Sue felt Mother stir beside her and answered quickly, before the argument could be stopped. "That was six months ago, Henry! It's all *over*."

"You'd better *hope* it's over!" Henry said. His eyes widened as he spoke, and he glanced out the window at the sheep barn.

"We all hope so," Mother said quietly. "In the meantime I agree with the girls. It's distressing to talk about. David, did you look at the currants this morning? Do you think they're ready?"

"It was distressing to *be* at!" Henry muttered. He was thinking of the animals, Sue knew, and she pushed her last slice of salt pork to the back of her plate. The fatty taste suddenly reminded her of the smell that lingered near the Campbells' barn.

Ed said, "Help you to some pie, sweet Sue?"

"Yes, please, rhubarb."

Mother glanced at her. "You should ask if anyone else wants it first."

Mother was only trying to hold Sue to her own standard. But if Clare had wanted the last slice of rhubarb pie, would Mother have said anything? Sue felt herself flush again.

Father reached across the table, took the rhubarb pie by its crisp rim of crust, and tipped it gently onto Sue's plate. He caught Mother's eye with a smile and a wink. "Boarding-house reach, Jane, I know. How will these youngsters learn manners if their old man doesn't show them any better?"

3

AFTER DINNER WASH THE DISHES and set the table again, plates and cups upside down on the scrubbed board.

"Let's take the sewing outdoors in the shade," Mother said, drying her hands on her apron. "Sue, will you bring chairs?" Sue nodded and pressed her lips tightly together to keep from sighing. "And then," Mother went on, "maybe you won't mind riding over to Ranney's to match this thread." She handed Sue a snip of Clare's green dress fabric, carefully wound around with a length of thread.

Clare could go to the White Mountains; Sue could go to Ranney's store. But it was *something.* She brought out the chairs and then ran upstairs. The red book bumped against her leg, and she remembered to thrust it deep under her pillow before changing.

Bright was in the barn. Mother liked to have a horse ready for errands, so each Morgan did farm work only half the day, and Father did most of his work with the big team.

Sue saddled and headed up the road in the shade of the big maples, listening to the scratch-scratch of the cultivators until the hill blocked the sound. At the town road she turned downhill, between other pastures and cornfields.

After a quarter mile the road passed between the Holdens'

11

house and barn, and a powerful smell of pig thickened the air. Jerome Holden, out yoking a team of his red oxen, called, "Hello, young Susan! Hot enough for you?"

"It's all of that!" Sue shouted. Mother would say to speak in a ladylike tone and that a simple yes would suffice. Sue's spirits began to rise. She trotted briskly around the corner onto the Westminster West road.

The Campbell mansion rose before her, long and many-windowed, its fluted white columns fronting the road. Bright pricked his ears at the heap of blackened timbers beside it, all that remained of the big barn. Sue made him walk. It would be like Bright to dump her in front of the only mansion in town.

But both of them would have liked to get past more quickly. The dead sheep and hogs had been removed, but the smell lingered, stronger now in the hot sun than it had been for several months. Bright danced, and his nostrils rattled lightly. Sue breathed through her mouth, the way Mother always told them not to, and thought she could taste something on the air.

Now they were past. Sue let Bright canter. He took this as permission to buck, too, and then swept on down the smooth, level road that ran for nearly a mile between small, flat fields. Then the road climbed a gentle slope and rounded a corner into the village—one street wide, between brook and pastures.

From the knoll overlooking the street the white church seemed to glance down, awakened by the clatter of Bright's hooves. Curtains were drawn aside, faces appeared, and old Reverend Stevens, driving his buggy and his neat bay horse, gave them a look of pure envy.

Sue dismounted in front of the store and led Bright to the

watering trough. He skimmed the surface of the water with his lips, took two breathy swallows, then stood gazing down the street, letting droplets fall back into the trough. A network of fine veins stood out on his hot shoulder. His nostrils were wide and red. Beautiful, Sue thought, as she tied him to the hitching post.

She started up the steps. Someone was speaking inside, a heavy, dogged male voice. "—let me have some flour against what Campbell's going to pay me."

"By rights, Johnny"—Alfred Ranney's voice—"what Campbell's paying you should go toward what you already owe."

"It's just money to you, Mr. Ranney. It's bread to Mother—"

Alfred Ranney let out a sigh as Sue pushed open the screen door. "Johnny, Lord knows I don't want to pester your father's widow, nor yet your father's son, but you got to find a way to start payin' me a little somethin'. There, we'll talk this over another time."

He turned. "Hello, Sue, what can I do you for?"

Sue stepped forward, a little reluctantly. "Mother sent me to match this thread."

Johnny Coombs glowered at her. He was in his early twenties, but his last hopeless attempt to gain something from his schooling had put him in the class with Ed and Henry. There was something clumsy and half finished about Johnny Coombs. He watched as Mr. Ranney found the green threads and compared them.

"Just take this to the window and make sure," Mr. Ranney suggested. Sue was happy to move away from the counter. Mothers all said to be kind to Johnny; he wasn't to blame for the way he was. Fathers tolerated him for the sake of *his* father, Tolman Coombs, who had been wounded in the war

13

and died just this winter of his hurts. But Johnny was easier to tolerate from a distance.

She held the two spools up to the light. "Yes, this is fine."

Mr. Ranney reached under the counter for the account book.

"If you're a *Gorham*, you can put things on account!" Johnny said. "If you're a *Campbell*, or a *Harlow*, or a *Goodhue*—"

"Johnny," Mr. Ranney interrupted. His voice sounded unnaturally patient. "Johnny, I know you're in a tight spot right now, and nobody wants to do you down. We'll talk to the overseer—"

"We aren't *poor!*" Johnny shouted. "Nor yet insane, so leave Goodhue out of it!"

Sue hurried down the steps, letting the quick drum of her boots drown out Johnny's voice. The overseer of the poor, Alfred Ranney had been about to say, and an able-bodied young man who owned a farm would resent—

"Susie!"

Sue turned, reins in hand. A buggy was coming up the street, drawn by a familiar chestnut horse. A light blue dress against the dark seat, a bonnet: "Minnie! Minnie Butler! When did you get home?"

"I came back Sunday, after church."

"Your folks didn't say anything about it!"

"They weren't expecting me," Minnie said. "Are you going right home?"

"Yes."

"Wait, I have to get a new mowing machine section, and we'll go together. Hold this horse!" Minnie dropped her reins on the dash and jumped out of the buggy. Sue took the chestnut's reins near the bit, pushing the inquisitive Bright away from him. She listened to Johnny Coombs's heavy voice break off again, a quick bit of chatter from Minnie, the clunk

14

of the iron section on the counter, and the big account book being dragged out again, then Minnie's steps on the stairs and Johnny Coombs: "If you're a *Butler*—"

"Phew! Wouldn't you know—the second person I run into in this town is *him!*" Minnie landed in the buggy with a jounce. "Do you want to tie Bright on behind or ride beside me?"

"I'll ride." Sue mounted, held Bright out of the way while Minnie turned the buggy, and then came up beside her. The buggy wheels rattled and puffed up the dust. Sue had to ride several feet away to avoid choking. They would have to shout, and as she realized that, Sue also realized that she didn't know what to say. Minnie had been working as hired girl on a farm north of Rockingham. She'd lived as a grown woman, away, and the jokes they used to share had been forgotten.

But Minnie didn't seem to feel that way. "Oh, it's good to be home!" she said. "And good to see you, Susie!"

"Didn't you like it up there?" Sue asked, cautiously, because with so many sisters Minnie had to work, and it didn't seem fair to raise the possibility of not liking it.

"It wasn't bad," Minnie said. "It's the same work you do at home, really. The only difference is you get paid for it."

"Didn't they give you all the hardest jobs?"

"Oh, I didn't mind that!" Minnie squared her shoulders. There was something she had minded—Sue could tell. But on the whole Minnie looked well; muscled, sturdy, with a bright, independent expression.

They were quiet for a moment. Then Minnie said, "It was the marriage proposals that wore *me* out!"

"*What?*" In her surprise Sue kicked Bright and had to bring him down from a trot. "The *what?*"

"Proposals of marriage. Night and day, Sue!"

"Did you accept?"

Minnie's eyes danced. "Susie, you should have *seen* him! Fifty years old if he's a day and washes his face on Sunday when he shaves! Weekdays he lets the tobacco juice build up amongst the chin whiskers. Oh, I was *sorely* tempted!"

"Who was this?"

"The hired man." Minnie made a face. "Hired man and hired girl. *He* couldn't see any difference between us, and it seemed like *they* couldn't either. So I said I shouldn't stay any longer, and I came home."

"Then they didn't treat you well."

"I don't call it treating a girl well to let her be bothered by a man like that. So I've taken a place with the Campbells, starting next week."

"Oh. I remember you saying once—"

"That I wouldn't work out near home, where everyone knows me? Hmmph!" Minnie tossed her head. "Near home they're likely to treat you with respect because they'll be seeing your folks in church on Sunday! My family's been in this town every bit as long as the Campbells. George Campbell made a fortune in wool, and that's the only difference!"

"It's a pretty fair difference!"

"Oh, but, Sue, you know what I mean! Nobody's any better than anybody else here in Westminster West. Julia Campbell may put on airs, but her mother's a Harlow, just like mine, and her grandmother's a Wilcox, like your mother. If you go out to work, Sue, don't you leave this town!"

Go *out* to work? I can be hired girl right at home! Sue thought.

They were nearing the Campbell place. On the back porch

16

someone shook dust out of a cloth. Bright stopped in his tracks and stared, blowing his breath out loudly. Then he sighed, as if to say Oh, well! and followed the plodding chestnut.

When Sue caught up, Minnie was craning her neck to look back at the blackened timbers of the big barn. "Tell me about the fires," she said. "Papa doesn't even want to talk about them, he's so scared, but I knew *you'd* tell! Your uncle Mathew Gorham was burned out, wasn't he?"

"Yes, in December, but nobody thought it was set. Then these barns burned, and it was obvious. All three of them were afire at once."

"Did you come over?"

"Father and Henry did—Ed was at the academy. They sent someone riding to call people. It looked like the house would go, too, for a while, but only one corner got scorched."

"Was there *really* a human skeleton in the ashes?" Minnie asked. "That's what I heard."

"No. People were saying that for a while. . . . But there were skeletons. Sheep—forty merinos—and hogs . . ." Henry and Father had come home looking sick at the suffering of the trapped animals.

"Don't say any more," Minnie said quietly. "No wonder Papa won't talk about it."

"Anyway," Sue said after a minute, "even if there was a human skeleton, it couldn't have been the firebug because the Drislanes' barn burned after that."

The voice shouting "fire" in the dooryard had had that Irish broadness, and Father said old Mother Drislane had stood on the front step watching the barn burn, tracing the sign of the cross over and over on her breast. All that hay gone up, oats, corn, calves . . .

17

"Stop thinking about it!" Minnie said. "You're looking green!"

Already they were at the Holdens'. It was a relief to pass between the solid, comfortable house and the big barn, as much a part of the landscape as Rocky Ridge or Windmill Hill. Barns were like that. They told of thrifty forebears and well-tended land, mellow soil, saving ways. But they were not as permanent as they looked.

4

AUNT MARY BRALEY was sewing with Mother and Clare when Sue reached home; Aunt Mary's bulk and black dress completely concealed the chair. "Hello, Sue," she called. "I been keepin' your seat warm!" She'd stopped on her way from her daughter's home in the East Parish, where she'd been nursing a grandaughter, the second to suffer from consumption.

As Sue brought another chair, Aunt Mary said, "I was happy I could spell Em'ly and let her get some rest, but 'twon't do any lasting good. Just tore my heart to see the poor child lay there day after day. *Prettiest* girl, and gets prettier the worse took she is. They do, you know—"

Mother cast a quick, worried glance at Clare.

"It's hard on Em'ly." Aunt Mary went on. "She'd come to depend on Ruby first, you know, and now that Laura's grown to where she's a help and comfort, *she's* . . ." Aunt Mary's voice failed. The tears rolled down her broad cheeks, but steadily, with only a little clumsiness, her old hands went on stitching. The afternoon felt suddenly much hotter.

"Has the minister been?" Mother asked.

"Yes, but . . . I shall ask Reverend Stevens to visit, too, if he gets over that way. It's not his parish, but he had my Em'ly in his Sunday school for fifteen years, and if there's

19

anyone likely to bring comfort, it's him. The sorrows *that* man has seen!"

"Yes," Mother said, folding away a piece of trim. "How anyone who's buried three wives could dare love a fourth! And on top of that, to lose both girls he adopted. But he means to take in a little boy, I understand."

"He has an open heart," Aunt Mary said soberly. "I didn't always think so. You remember, don't you, Jane, that sermon he preached when poor Walter Ranney was killed at Gettysburg?"

Mother nodded slowly, and Sue's interest perked up. She would rather hear about war than sickness.

"I was crying my eyes out," Aunt Mary said. "Well, most of us had somebody of our own to worry about down there, besides grievin' for poor Walter. And then Reverend Stevens as much as said it didn't matter he was killed! The nation had sinned, and it had to pay in blood. Oh, that made me mad! Because *Walter* didn't sin! He never bought nor sold any black people!"

"Reverend Stevens also said that Walter expected hardship," Mother said quietly.

"Yes. Well, what you expect up here to home and what it's really like once you get into it are two different things! A lot of them found that out! But you're right, Jane. He took a harder view of the war than some, but you can't doubt his good heart or his faith. He'll have some good words for my Em'ly—and me, too, I expect." She wiped her eyes with the back of her hand and stood up. "Seems as if all I've got to offer is tribulation talk, so I'll take my leave of you young ladies."

Mother walked her to the buggy. Aunt Mary untied the horse and hoisted herself into the buggy, giving it a pronounced list to the right. Mother stood with her hand on the wheel. She and Aunt Mary seemed to speak very seriously, very privately.

"It's too bad about her grandaughter," Sue said.

Clare let her hands rest in her lap for a moment. The needle stood out sharp and dark against the white lace. She looked off toward the cornfield, as if she saw something dreadful and fascinating. "It's true," she said after a moment. "They get more and more lovely."

For a moment the romantic image caught Sue, too: the face blazing in brief beauty on a white pillow; the ethereal slenderness, changing a young woman into something like an angel—

She glanced up to see a rapt, excited look on Clare's face, and something squeezed in her chest: fear, annoyance, or both. "Well, *you* aren't consumptive!" she said. "And I don't believe it's all that beautiful when the blood starts pouring out of their mouths!"

Clare flushed and took up her mending again. "You're so refined, Sue!"

There's nothing refined about *really* being sick, Sue wanted to say. But Mother was coming back, and Mother did not allow them to quarrel. Sue gripped her lips together and stabbed her needle through the fabric. Of course Clare was attracted to sickness. Look what it had done for her already!

Supper, and supper dishes. When they were done and the table was set for breakfast, it was still light out. Father hitched Bright to the buggy. He was going to see Homer Goodhue on town business, and Mother was riding with him.

Clare lay in the hammock with a book, giving the impression of being dressed in white, though she wore calico just like Sue. Henry was on the lawn, reading *The Agriculturalist*, and Ed sat with his sketchbook on his knees, drawing the barn.

"We'll be home by dark," Mother called as Bright set off briskly downhill and along the edge of the big cornfield. Sue stood feeling the late sun hot on her cheek, following them in her mind, over the brook and down the tiny back road. She would have liked to go with them—go anywhere!

"Ed!"

"Susie!" Ed tossed his pencil up and caught it in midair.

"Let's go swimming!"

"All right, let's! You two want to come?"

Henry turned a page and shook his head. Clare looked tempted for a moment. She sat up straight in the hammock, reminding Sue of the wild games they used to play in it: train wreck, earthquake.

"Come on!" Sue meant to urge playfully, but irritation came through in her voice, and Clare lay back again.

The ice pond was behind the house, across the narrow dogleg of cornfield that ran between the buildings and the brook. Ed was already shrugging off his suspenders as he reached the bank. Sue struggled with her buttons. Clare should have been there, to hurry them along.

I miss Clare, Sue thought. They used to fight like boys sometimes. Clare had given her a black eye. She had knocked out one of Clare's baby teeth. They used to be so alike, and they'd always wanted the same thing.

Ed waded into the water as Sue undid her last button and let her dress fall around her feet. She stepped out of it, cool in her thin summer shift, and went down the slope. Lonely. That was how she felt. Lonely, bored, overworked—

"Aaagh! Ed, you pig! Quit splashing!"

"Make me!" Ed taunted, splashing again.

Sue waded into the water, taking big, slow strides against its pressure. Ed swam away on his back, laughing. "Can't catch me! Can't—" Sue plunged and seized him by the ankle. He went under and came up coughing. "Susie! Be gentle! Be womanly! If you're not slower than me, at least pretend!"

"I haven't drowned you nearly enough," Sue said. "You're still talking!"

Instantly Ed glided away, silent as a water bug, hands and feet never breaking the surface. Sue followed his example. The water stilled, caught the last red in the evening sky. Sue watched the ripples spread, full of color and shadow. It would be wonderful to be a painter with talent enough to capture this. Not even Ed could do that, not yet.

But why paint the water when the water was here? And why draw the barn when the barn was there, as solid as the hill?

Why do anything, really? You planted and preserved and cooked because the food kept getting eaten. There was no more interesting reason. You visited and gossiped to exchange the news. But in a group of families that had shared one narrow valley for a hundred years, how much news could there be? You went to church to learn about God and be kept from sin. But was there really much scope for sin in Westminster West? Everyone followed in the track worn by the previous generation, as cows follow one another across a hillside. Even Ed, leaving in January for music school, was following a pattern. The people whose lives took unexpected turns were those who had gone out into the wider world.

"Is that why you're leaving, Ed?"

"Is what why? Brr! I'm getting out." Ed clambered up the

bank, his underdrawers hanging in heavy, dripping folds. He picked up his shirt and pants and disappeared behind a bush. Sue chose another bush. "Is what why?" Ed repeated.

"Because—because it's so dull here!" The shift dropped to her feet. Sue stood shivering in the twilight, hoping to dry off a little before struggling into her dress.

"No, I'm leaving because I love to sing and I can't be a singer in Westminster West. But I don't think it's *dull*. Do you?"

"It's easy not to think it's dull when you've spent the last three winters away!" Sue said. Ed laughed. "But really, has anything truly *astonishing* ever happened here?"

"Susie, you read too many newspapers!" Sue could hear him fighting into his clothes. She let her dress drop over her head, pulled it down where it stuck to her skin, then reached back for the buttons. "Tragic shipwreck!" Ed was intoning. "Train derailment! Man murders wife and children! Western outlaws rob bank!"

"No," Sue said, "the biggest excitement we've had is the barn fires, and we'll be talking about them for the next hundred years. At least Henry will!"

They started toward the house. The sky was a deep violet now. Far across the cornfield Bright skimmed along, his step as fresh and eager as if he'd stood in his stall all day.

"Mother will say we could have caught a cramp," Sue said, "and then she'll say, 'Wring those wet things out before you hang them up, Sue.' Doesn't it ever *bother* you that you know just what's going to happen next?"

"But that's like music," Ed said. "You can tell where music is going, but that doesn't mean it's not beautiful."

"It doesn't mean it *is*, either!"

Ed didn't say anything more, only whistled softly to himself as they climbed the slope. Mother was just getting down from the buggy. Sue tried to hide her wet shift, but Mother clicked her tongue.

"Swimming right after supper! You could have caught a cramp! Sue, will you—Young man, just what are you laughing about?"

Inside, Ed went to the piano, drawing them all with him. It was nearly eleven when they scattered for bed.

Piano notes echoed in Sue's head as she slipped between the cool sheets. She reached up to adjust the pillow, and her fingers struck something hard. The red book.

The music had smoothed out Sue's hot, prickly feelings, but touching the book took her straight back to the attic. She flexed her finger, trying to make it hurt. Then she turned the lamp up brighter and cracked the book open to the first page. It was dated at the top: July 18, 1865.

5

July 18, 1865. Home. Father drove me up from Bratt.
this evening. What would he have felt, could he read
my thoughts as I sat beside him, silent, behind the slow
old horse? The wheels turning, turning, and all
through Putney village the houses, lit up and glowing
like paper lanterns. Tears came to my eyes. So much
beauty, so much peace. It seems impossible that this
has been here all this long time.

Yet I am not peaceful. Passing those quiet houses,
seeing a woman within, the balance of skirts,
dishes on the table, I trembled, and felt myself the
Enemy.

Dear old Father's affection was almost motherly,
Mother's everything a mother's can be. But so aged—
and the house so hot, so full! I was greatly relieved to
be free of them after supper, escape to my room, fling
open the window and breathe!

I have been longing to see them, so many months.
How soon must I see Jane, and will I feel the same?

Jul. 19. Cultivated 3 acres. Father said rest, but of course
I could not. His hands shook on the harness buckles,
and I could have wept. I walked behind old Pete all day,
and with every step I felt I dragged a chain. We have

died in our thousands to free the Negro. How many of us have gone home to freedom?

Jul. 20. Cultivated.

Jul. 21. Cultivated and mended harness, helped Father clean out the calf pen. He does not know how to speak to me, nor I to him. He remembers that I have obeyed the orders of captains and majors and doesn't give orders himself, only timid suggestions. I try to guess what he wants. Found myself longing today for the freedom of the campfire and a tin cup full of Oh Be Joyful.
   Wish I did not feel compelled to write this all down. If Mother finds this, I don't know what it will do to her.

Jul. 22. Church tomorrow. Polished my boots and brushed my coat this evening—trembling as we once did on the eve of battle. But then each of us knew. We laughed and drank and were quiet together—no need to speak of why. Tonight I watched Mother nod over her stitching beside the stove, while Father so carefully polished his boots over a sheet of the Gazette, lest a single drop stain that scrubbed floor. I thought of Dana and Jim Thorne, heading west even now. Would that I were with them!

Jul. 24. Cultivated. Bad headache. Mother knows, I believe, in spite of all my caution. I have seen her eyes on me all day, grieved. Drunken, and on Sunday! I have done worse, but of that she knows nothing.

Jul. 25. Today we mowed, and I was pleased to see Father's firm, steady step. He worked all day long and seemed as hardened a marcher as I. Indeed I fell behind. My skill is much diminished. He was pleased, I think, to be able to instruct me at last.

Jul. 26. Hall stopped as we sat down to dinner, to say that poor Buxton is returned from Andersonville. It does not seem possible that he can live.

I thought H. looked at me very closely throughout the meal. Louisa is Jane's dearest friend and I'm sure is often with her just now. I have behaved badly. I know it—perhaps the whole village knows it now. But when I saw her pale face turn toward me, with that mild, sweet expression, I could not bear it. I am no longer worthy. Was I ever? I don't know, but certainly am not now. My great fear is that I no longer wish to be.

Jul. 27. Terrible. Scything thistle in the sheep pasture with Father—he has let the weeds grow up very much in the past four years. Asters, goldenrod, and thistles very thick—

Again my skill was less than his but not so bad. We worked along in the sun, and the weeds tumbled down over the blade. Was it sweat in my eyes? The weeds as they fell began to look like soldiers. I have seen them fall just like that, as easily. Just as today I scythed weeds, once I scythed men down. I began to see their faces, and all at once I was weeping. When I sobbed aloud, Father turned to see. Then we sat in the shade beside the spring, his arm around my shoulders. But I could tell him little. At last he concluded it was the sun, a weakness brought on by exposure to the Southern climate.

My trouble was contracted in the South, but not from sun. Its very opposite!

28

Jul. 28. Last night awakened Mother and Father with a loud shout. Dreaming, apparently. I don't remember.

Jul. 29. Again. Mother greatly distressed, refused to tell me what I had said or in what manner I cried out.

Church again tomorrow. I must do better this time. I learned to face Rebel fire. That was because of the press behind me, the friends around me, each fearing that he would break. I will think of Hall's eyes upon me—all their eyes. They are all watching.

Jul. 30. Awoke weeping. I dreamed I slept on the battlefield, with my blanket around my ears to drown out the dying groans and the shrieks of the wounded. The dreadful sound, the stench in my nostrils, and the aching knowledge in my heart that some of those groaning were dear friends—yet I must sleep. Mother looked very tired this morning and got a little burn on her hand as she made breakfast.

At the church door I felt very sick. Nearly excused myself. But at the last moment saw Peter Davis in the pew ahead. His head was up in that gallant way he has, yet I knew from our drunken talk last week that he feels much as I do. I marched resolutely past him, and he winked at me! Glad to report that when he proposed a repeat of last week's debauch, I declined. Eliza Coombs there with her little boy—Tolman's wound still troubles him very much.

Afterward I was not able to avoid Jane. Her meek, bowed head was a reproach to me all through the service. Yet after, when the press brought me near her, she flushed and turned from me sharply. She is angry—and that lightens my heart inexplicably. I spoke a word to her, but she answered very coldly and moved away, leaving me to watch in mingled hurt and satisfaction.

Midnight. Can I settle here, and take up this life again? I must—or perhaps it will kill me. To think that these fields once seemed so wide! All day I felt the hills closing around me, and at evening, when I stood washing at the pump, I thought I saw the broad field before the house filled up with an army. Only it would not accommodate the tenth part of an army! I thought I saw men running through the corn, crushing and trampling it. How the dirt would fly and the valley fill with thunder! All evening in my mind I set defenses around the house, and now I sit up, every sense straining. Insane! A mile away, is Peter sitting up, too? Or does he drink himself to sleep at night? And poor Buxton, lying on his bed—Hall was by; he tells us the poor fellow is just clinging to life—does he, too, keep awake for his watch? Does he hear the clink of the bits, the thud of hooves, as I do?

Imagine—they think we will sink back into our lives as before, court the nice girls we courted once, and settle down to farming! If Mother would only explain to Jane, very kindly and simply, about the screaming and the weeping in the night, if someone would show her the lamp burning long past midnight, it might ease her mind somewhat.

Reverend S. might undertake this for me—a man who understands women. The current incumbent at the parsonage is the third Mrs. S.

July 31. A party up to Hall's. Peter has felt himself equal to the occasion, and Miss Louisa has got him at last! Awkward—Jane there, and every eye upon us. A similar

event was certainly expected on our account, only a
few years ago. Jane has passed those years unchanged.
I do think her as good and lovely as ever. But as for
myself—I actually blush when I consider the kind of
thing I once said to her, the easy, gushing sentiment. I
feel I might be the grandfather of that boy—and I want
nothing more than to kick him in the pants, burn down
house, barn, and crops, and head for the West!

What is Jane intending? I thought she flirted with
Goodhue in hopes of reawakening my feelings, but
perhaps I flatter myself. He is a widower, well
established—land poorer than this, and his farming
practices antiquated, but she may not care for that. But
so stooped and grizzled. I actually shuddered when I
thought of them together. I at least am whole in body
and not disgusting to look on—so I've been told!
Perhaps J. can see within, however. Her eyes are more
piercing than I ever thought them. Who knows—
perhaps she would jilt me, if given the chance.

Aug. 1. Throat ached half the day. I dreamed of us
stacking arms, when we were mustered out of the
army. Apparently I did not weep aloud, for no questions
this morning, and no grieved looks. Helped Mother
haul water for the washing, and one of Allen's girls came
up to work with her, as she's been doing since Laura
married. Since I have added my own clothing and linen
to this burden, perhaps I should contribute a wife to
help bear it. Mother quite exhausted at the end of the
day. I demonstrated my skill at rough-and-ready
cooking and made an evening meal that horrified her.

Aug. 2. Old Spot calved this noon, needed some
assistance. Thought I would actually faint at the sight.
The blood and the groans—I was back on the battlefield,

31

holding Gage in my arms as he died, watching
someone's head blown off. Who was that? I can't
remember, except that I did know him, and I never
wept a tear, just charged on with all the rest. Already
I can hardly comprehend how we did that, but I
remember that I did not fear. In action fear vanishes.
Mother would say I saved it up for later!

The calf this evening was curled up like a dog, her
red coat shining. Looked so new and lovely that tears
came to my eyes.

Aug. 3. The Reverend S. and his wife dined with us
today. The courage of these women to keep on
wedding him. More certain death than in any charge I
ever saw—100% losses to date!

Walked with me afterward, to smoke a pipe of sweet
tobacco and talk. He tried very gently to draw me
out—sent on Jane's behalf? I found it impossible to
respond. He is good and intelligent, and I do respect him,
but he, like all the rest, is trying to squeeze me back
into the old mold. I have expanded beyond it—for ill
as well as good. I've been enlarged, and the changes
hardened into my nature by searing fire. That is the
whole of my problem, and he bears some responsibility,
for it was his zeal, his preaching that sent us all forth.

He tells me there is some talk of Jane going West.
She has taught school here and could do it there—
but does she understand the dangers?

Aug. 4. Thought of the West continually today. A soldier
can get land out there for almost nothing.

But I have land here, good land. Here or there I'll be
hitched to the same plow. More sensible to stay where
I don't have to bust sod and fight Indians.

32

Long argument this evening with Father on the subject of fertilizers. He has kept up well with the times in his use of equipment, I'll grant, but he hasn't an idea in the world about fertilizer! Mother sat and smiled over her knitting. When I questioned her, she said, "Go on, dear. It's as good as a play."

Aug. 5. Dreaming again. They were charging us and we were firing. My rifle worked more smoothly and swiftly than ever in life. It smoked and bucked in my hands. I saw the red blossom on their faces, on their coats and shirts—fewer and fewer of them to come on, until finally none were left. We stood up from our guns, we looked, and we were all weeping. "Aren't there any more?" I asked. "Won't they come again?" But all of them lay dead on the field; there was no movement in the trees to show us an army remained.

Aug. 6. Church again. Old Cynthia Tuthill died this morning—Rev. S. attended the deathbed, came in late and disheveled to service. They will bury her tomorrow afternoon. Came on to rain this evening, looks as if it will rain all night.

August 7. "What do you think I am?" Jane turned at her gate and asked me that, with such an expression— I am utterly bewildered, must go back and find my way through the afternoon, step by step.
After dinner we washed and put on church clothes, drove to the village for Cynthia Tuthill's service. I kept thinking of all the poor fellows shoveled into southern holes with hardly a word said over them. Old lady Tuthill's single death barely crossed my mind.
Stayed at the back of the crowd, but the sound of

33

shoveling still reached me. When we all turned away, somehow Jane was beside me. Accident, her design, a conspiracy of the entire village? I hardly know, but I felt I must escort her home. She had walked, of course; her parents, both infirm now, came in the buggy.

It felt impossible to speak at first. Nothing could have been more public. Her veil hid her face, but I felt she was not lifting her eyes to notice me.

At last I thought I might put her expectations to rest, assure her that the fault lay all with me. I stammered out a few words—I hardly know what: dreams, the nervous strain, a mental confusion that made me unfit for female society. She listened to me in the most appalling silence. Then we reached their front gate. She opened the latch, I thought she would go inside without a word. But she turned as if she must speak, pushing back her veil. Her face so fierce that I really did jump. "What do you think I am?" she asked me. And not waiting for an answer, she swept inside and positively slammed the door.

The clock has just tolled one.

"What do you think I am?"

Downstairs the clock tolled one.

The sound spread a long, slow shiver down Sue's back and through the silent house. The curtains stirred at the window, and the breeze smelled like rain. "What do you think I am?" She turned the page. There must be more. It couldn't end here.

But all the remaining pages were blank. "What do you think I am?" and then nothing, as if that question had so puzzled the writer that it suspended all other thoughts.

34

She turned back to the beginning. Her fingers trembled, making the stiff old paper rattle. She saw a ridge near the spine of the book, remnant of earlier pages that had been neatly sliced out with a knife. The short ends of the pages were flecked with brown ink, spattered with the beginnings of words. "I," she read, and "br," "sh," "G," "L." What she had just read had to be hidden. What had come before must have been even worse; it was destroyed.

The lamplight made a warm yellow circle that included most of the room. But the corners were deeply shadowed, and black shadows at the edge of every object—chair, washstand, closet door—seemed to add an extra dimension. Sue could feel her heartbeat rock her body: bump-bump, bump-bump.

Everything she'd known all day was not true. The uniform and wedding dress embracing in the trunk; the gallant young soldier and the maid who waited for him—they were not the real story, just as the sad, sweet songs they'd sung this evening and the war reminiscences in the newspaper were not real. They were like the pictures in *Harper's*, where all the horses' legs moved in unison, like the fashion models in *Godey's*, with waists as thin as their necks.

What else was not true?

Father. Second selectman, prominent and solid citizen of Westminster West. Father, the embodiment of the town, as much as any Goodhue or Harlow or Alfred Stevens himself. Father, the man of few and plain words. Father, as prosaic as a salt shaker . . .

Father, who had wanted only to leave, ". . . burn down house, barn, and crops." Wept at the sight of a new red calf. Drank on Sunday. Tried to jilt his sweetheart.

With a sigh and a whisper the rain started. The lamp began

to run out of oil. The circle of light contracted, and the shadows in the corners grew. Then with a little gasp the flame puffed out. The room went black, and the silvery gauze curtains shifted and stirred.

Bong! said the clock. One-thirty. Sue couldn't remember that she'd ever stayed up this late. The house was a shell of silence within the noisy, raining night, and her eyes were wide open. She felt as if she might never sleep again.

6

"GOODNESS, CHILD, you look like death warmed over!"

Mother's eyes *were* piercing, even early in the morning. Sue turned away to grind the coffee. She had slept a little. Two-thirty the clock had chimed, and she didn't remember three. Now it was six o'clock, perfectly light out, Henry coming to the door with milk pails, bacon in the pan. Every time footsteps sounded at the door, Sue looked to see if it was Father. She felt as if she'd never seen him in her life.

". . . somebody who's a farmer!" Henry again, bringing the last milk pails. "Hasn't anything burned since winter, has it? It's somebody that's too cussed busy, come spring, to do anything but work. Give him a minute's breather, and he'll be at it again!"

"Barns do burn, Henry, without anybody setting fire to them." That was Ed, pausing at the door to pry off his boots before he carried his two pails to the pantry. Henry handed his pails to Sue. Their weight stretched her shoulders—into the pantry, where Ed lifted them into the spring box.

"Quick's we get that corn cultivated—" Father's voice. Heat flooded Sue's face. It was like the time she had walked in on him bathing and seen him naked. He didn't know about that, either. . . . She turned and peeked out the pantry door.

He looked exactly as he always did. He looked like Father.

Sue blinked hard. Her eyes were dry this morning, but it was more than that; a pattern intervened and kept her from really seeing. A set of knowledge told her: This is Father. He's eager to start mowing, thinks Henry is funny talking about the fires again, likes the smell of bacon, will sit down, yes, and rub his hands together in the eager way that means he's in a happy frame of mind. . . .

Does it?

Father seemed so simple on the surface, but that wasn't true. His correct, dutiful, matter-of-fact responses to life— so staunch, so *Father*-like—were not Father. Not all of him.

When had he started to like his life again? *Did* he like his life? Did Westminster West become big enough to contain the boy who had seen a war?

"Sue?" Mother paused in her quick stepping around to lay her wrist against Sue's forehead. "No fever. Goodness, child, brisk up! You're as bad as Clare this morning!"

The morning passed in a haze—a real haze, as the hot sun cooked the juices out of the earth, and an inner haze, which seemed to come between Sue's eyes and her understanding. Even her busy hands, which picked currants until her fingers were red and stinging from the juice, which stemmed the currants, bagged them in cheesecloth, stirred them into brilliant red jelly on the stove in the summer kitchen, and squeezed the last juice out of the bag, seemed far away and not connected to her mind.

Dinner. It was impossible, after all, to look at Father. She would glance up, see the shape of his long nose and the crosshatched lines beside his eyes and then away, knowing nothing more than before.

Listening was easier, but how little Father said! Sue kept needing to glance up to see what he was thinking, and the hot, miserable blush would rise. I don't like this, she thought, bending low over her plate. She would put the book back. She would never think about it again—

"I need a chicken killed for Sunday dinner," Mother remarked. "And Henry, could you mend this table before you go back out? The leaf is sagging terribly."

"All right," Henry said.

Ed made a face. "Then I'll have to do in the bird. Unless you will, Captain?" He made his mouth innocent, but his eyes teased.

Father's silence seemed to deepen, and Mother cast Ed a warning look. Father never butchered anything. Mother killed the hens if neither boy was around, or sometimes Sue did. When a hog or sheep was butchered, George Corey came to do it, and Father left for the day. Sue had never wondered why. That was just Father. Now she could think of reasons.

Ed said, "Okay. Point out your victim, Mother dear, and she'll go to the block!"

"Thank you, Ed. Then Sue can pluck and draw the bird while I—"

"Mother," Clare said, "do we have to talk about this at the dinner table?"

At the same instant Sue found herself saying, "Mother, may I do the pies instead?"

Mother looked bewildered for an instant, attention divided between Sue and Clare. It was Sue she settled on this time. "You mustn't let yourself start to get squeamish, Sue. These jobs have to be done."

The word *squeamish* was almost Sue's undoing. It brought to mind the warmth of the innards, the heavy smell. Her stomach nearly heaved. That must be the smell of the battle-field, too.

Mother eyed her sharply. "All right. This time you may do the pies."

As they washed dishes, Sue tried not to hear the squawk of the captured hen, the thunk of the ax striking the chopping block, and the scuffle as the hen's body struggled in the grass with no head. Clare avoided the sounds easily, sitting in the rocker with her fingers in her ears. Far down the field the scratch of the cultivator would drown the sound for Father.

"Hey, Sue!" Henry called. "Will you look at the level?"

The spirit level, a polished length of hardwood with brass ends, lay across from table to leaf. Sue looked at the glass tube embedded in one long edge. A bubble floated in yellow liquid, and when the bubble settled between two lines on the tube, the table was level. "Not yet," she said.

Henry added a shim. Sue watched the bubble tremble and drift. Something seemed adrift inside her, too, and the tremor of the spirit level set up a sympathetic tremor in her stomach. She almost felt sick.

7

SUE READ THE DIARY twice through that night. On Sunday morning her eyes prickled with tiredness. The light seemed too much for them, and when she had strained her corset shut, it squeezed her so tightly she could barely breathe. She blinked hard to chase the black dots from her vision, finished dressing, and went downstairs to the hot kitchen.

Father changed his clothes and showed himself to Mother. "Neat and respectable, Jane?"

It was Westminster West's Sunday joke. Reverend Stevens had once presented himself to his wife for before-church inspection. Sue could picture Mrs. Stevens looking at him in that bland, complacent way that masked her sense of fun.

"Your coat, your collar, and necktie look very nice and neat. But, Alfred, you would look much neater and more respectable if you wore a pair of trousers!"

The same joke every Sunday. The same seats in the wagon, same journey, same road. Just past the corner of Westminster West road, the same call from behind.

"Hello there, Gorhams. I need to pass."

That was Deacon Buxton— "poor Buxton," who'd been a prisoner at Andersonville—driving his wife and two children behind a thin team. Father firmed his hands on the reins as the deacon passed. Bright and Lucky were apt to think it was a race.

After Deacon Buxton came the Millers, late in starting and driving fast to make up for it, their five boys and two girls piled in the spring wagon. Bright and Lucky swelled their necks, asking for more rein. Father let the leather slide through his hands, and Sue felt the surge of power in the wagon. Of course it was not a race, but though they were the best of friends, Father never did like to let Reuben Miller pass him.

A Sunday like every other.

But Sue felt a doubleness, another Sunday shadowing this one. Father had set out on this same road, with new-blacked boots and dread in his heart, past the same landmarks in the same wagon, behind old Queen, who was Bright and Lucky's granddam. If some magic had given Sue the ability to see both Sunday journeys at once, it would be like a stereoscope: two flat pictures, nearly identical, jumping into three-dimensionality.

At church Ed went up the aisle with Mother on his arm. Sue and Clare followed, side by side. Sun streamed through the tall windows, across the assembled bonnets and bowed gray heads, the worn coats, the shiny black of good Sunday dresses. The pattern blurred past Sue's eyes, making her slightly dizzy. She was grateful to sink onto the wooden seat of the Gorham pew, as familiar and homelike as any room in their house.

Ed took his place with the singers, Father and Henry came in from stabling the horses, and Reverend Stevens advanced to the pulpit. Voices were lifted in song, Ed's rich baritone underlying, leading, and supporting.

Then Reverend Stevens opened his sermon and embarked on his leisurely course, its firstlys, secondlys, and thirdlys providing the Sunday rhythm that had been the same for

42

more than forty years. Flies droned. Fans rustled. A sudden scent of horehound betrayed some worried cougher.

He never mentions the war, Sue realized. Not even in his fortieth anniversary address last year, when he'd listed where each person sat on the morning of his first sermon. Once he'd been passionate about the war. Now he was as silent on the subject as he was about his three dead wives. The war's wreckage was before him: Otis Buxton, too thin to look at; George Harlow, who wept at certain songs; Father. And Tolman Coombs, now dead, who had always seemed so watchful and so completely passive. But thoughts, everyone's thoughts, are hidden, and Alfred Stevens concealed his perfectly behind his firm, plain, manly face.

Afterward, in the churchyard, everyone began to speak at once, softly at first, then louder, to be heard above the rising voices. Sue paused on the steps, trying to breathe against the press of her corset, trying to see through the brightness. Coats, white shirts crossed by suspenders, black satin stretched shiny across stiff waists and swirled like patterns in a kaleidoscope.

Faces—Ranney, Gorham, Harlow, Goodell—smiled, turned, smiled again. Only a few faces didn't seem to fit: young men who were farm workers and came from somewhere else. Alonzo Codding and Charlie West each had a round-cheeked look, a hat-on-the-back-of-the-head look, even on Sunday.

Julia Campbell swished past Sue, leaving a heavy perfume on the air. The sunlight glinted in her golden ringlets, and suddenly Clare appeared at her side. "Julia! We're working on my traveling dress now! Are *you* ready?"

"Oh, I suppose so," Julia answered carelessly, scanning the crowd.

Clare turned to look, too, leaving Sue a view of their hats—songbird's wings on Julia's, velvet and false pearls on Clare's. "I know," Clare said. "Isn't fitting a *bore*? But soon we'll be *away*—"

"Susan, dear, come over into the shade." A soft, smooth hand closed over Sue's. Delyra Goodhue's pretty, faded face smiled up at her.

"I know just how you feel," Mrs. Goodhue said, guiding Sue gently down the steps. In a moment they were free of the crowd, standing apart under the shade of the elms. It was flattering to be noticed by Delyra Goodhue. It was Westminster West's famous romance. Homer Goodhue had left to make his fortune, and for twenty-three years Delyra Tuthill waited for him. By the time he returned she was an invalid, but the wedding went forward, and there could be no doubt of their happiness.

"Here, dear." Delyra fumbled in her bag and handed Sue a peppermint. "Church in the summertime *is* a strain." She waved her fan with a delicate, gentle motion. Sue almost reached for it, to make a more robust breeze for them both. But Delyra Goodhue made her feel big and bumptious, and it was better to stay still.

"Sue!" Mother appeared beside them. "There you are!"

"Sue seemed a little overcome, Janey," Mrs. Goodhue said. "I've been feeding her peppermints." A flap of the fan sent another small puff of air across Sue's face. She felt herself blush. She hadn't been overcome, exactly. But it would be rude to contradict.

"There, Jane. See how her color comes and goes? I don't like the look of that."

Mother didn't seem to want to discuss Sue's color. She

44

turned as Johnny Coombs drove past in his rusty buggy pulled by a plowhorse. His mother leaned back against the cushions, a bluish tint to her lips.

"I must visit her once the preserves are finished." Mother said, as if to herself.

"You'll want to choose a time when Johnny's out," Delyra Goodhue said. She sounded suddenly brisk and sharp. "Eliza's perfectly accepting of a little present now and then, but Johnny doesn't want her to have anything he hasn't gotten her himself."

Slowly Mother shook her head. "I do think there's times when property's a millstone. If Johnny didn't have a few acres holding him, I suppose he'd go west and find some sort of place for himself."

"He's working for Fred Campbell," Delyra Goodhue said, "siding that new hay barn on the hill. So one good thing's come of the fires; they're putting bread on poor Eliza's table!"

Father came with the wagon, and it was down the dusty road again, with plenty to talk about. A singing school was starting in the fall. Susie Leach, who'd been to Europe, would give a talk at the parsonage. A cornet band in the East Parish . . .

"In my young days we'd talk over the sermon occasionally," Mother remarked, looking back at them and looking hardest at Sue, who'd said nothing.

"Ahoy there!" Ed said suddenly. "Accident!" At the corner of Perry Hill Road a buggy tilted, axle broken. A sweating gray farm horse stood anxiously in the shafts, while Johnny Coombs climbed out over the steep angle of the dash. Little Mrs. Coombs perched on the high end of the seat.

"Slow down there, Johnny, we'll give you a hand," Henry said.

Johnny scowled and hoisted his mother out with one arm,

holding the reins in his free hand. Mrs. Coombs's skirt caught. There was a glimpse of shoe and stocking and a ripping sound. For one moment her face, over his shoulder, looked scared and appealing. Then color rose faintly in her cheeks. He set her down, and she turned away, as Johnny bent to look at his axle.

"Ed, hop down and hand Eliza up here beside me," Mother said quickly. "We'll drive her home, and you boys can help Johnny fix his buggy."

But when Ed offered Mrs. Coombs his arm, Johnny swung around, fists clenched. "I'll take care of her!"

"Now, Johnny—" Ed sounded soothing.

"Don't you 'Now, Johnny' me!" Johnny stepped forward, his bull shoulders humped. He looked huge.

Sue's heart thudded almost painfully. She leaned forward, ready to snatch the whip from its socket. She felt Clare's hand clutch her arm.

Henry stepped between Johnny and Ed. "Johnny," he said, in a voice so careful that it sounded dull. "Johnny, my folks'll take your mother home. Let's have a look at that buggy."

Johnny's eyes remained fixed on Henry's face. Sue couldn't look away, but in the blurred edge of her vision she sensed Ed quietly leading Mrs. Coombs to the wagon, helping her up.

Then Ed turned back to Johnny and Henry, an extra little spring in his step and a sway to his shoulders. Father grunted softly and almost spoke.

"Well, Johnny," Ed said. "How about it?"

Sue could hear Johnny's harsh breathing. He seemed to bulk even larger, big enough to take care of Ed and Henry both.

46

He laughed.

It was like coming down a flight of stairs and missing the last step. "Don't think there's much to do but move 'er off the road and unhitch," he said, and bent to the axle again. The back of his neck was brick red.

Henry and Ed looked at each other, shrugged, and joined him. Father let out his breath in a quiet sigh and shook the reins over the horses' backs.

Climbing Perry Hill was like entering a different, poorer country. The soil grew rocky. Houses were small, unpainted. One was abandoned, a gray shell with black windows like empty, eyeless sockets. Lilacs grew around a cellar hole. Samuel Shattuck, who had not crossed the church threshold since the pews were turned around fifteen years before, could be seen out mowing hay with a scythe.

Bright and Lucky leaned into the breast collars, and they passed the Shattuck field slowly. Sue had a long chance to watch old Sam mowing, the step-and-sweep rhythm, the tall grass tumbling over the blade ". . . like soldiers. I have seen them fall just like that, as easily."

The motion of the wagon was beginning to make Sue feel sick. Up the steep hill . . . Here was the exact spot where forty years ago Homer Miller had been killed by his father's dump cart. Bela Miller was picking up stones to work out his road tax. As the cart grew heavier, it pushed the steers, making them reluctant to stand. Bela told ten-year-old Homer to stand in front of them.

Sue had heard the story many times, but never had she imagined it so vividly. The sullen steers tossed their heads, ears flicking back toward the load that became heavier with every rock added by the father. The first step would be barely intended, but it made bracing impossible. It allowed the cart full of stones to push and push, and the little boy in front was too stubborn or too obedient to move. Maybe he thought he could stop them. Up until the wheel ran over his body, maybe he thought it would be all right.

"Father?" Sue touched his hard shoulder. "Stop? I'm going to—"

"*Ugh!*" said Clare, barely audibly. But as Sue bent, retching, over the side of the wagon, she felt Clare's warm hand on her back.

Mother turned on the wagon seat, looking over Mrs. Coombs's threadbare shoulder. "So that's why you've been looking so peaked," she said. "Peppermint tea when we get home, young lady, and then bed!"

8

WHITE PILLOW COOL AND FIRM under her head. Cool white sheet drawn up under her chin. Window shades pulled halfway down, white gauze curtains stirring softly in the afternoon breeze.

It was a great satisfaction to lie still. The moment of danger was past.

The danger had been Mother, bringing Sue upstairs with an arm around her waist, helping her sit on the edge of the bed, and reaching to plump the pillow. Under that pillow was the red book.

It had been instinct: the realistic, convincing noise in her throat, the falling a little forward, one hand to her mouth. "Oh, my goodness!" And Mother was bending to look beneath the bed for the chamber pot. In the moment it took for her to find it, Sue drew the book from under the pillow and slipped it beneath her thigh.

"*Here,*" Mother said urgently, and for a moment Sue thought she might actually need the chamber pot. But the nausea passed.

"I'll get your nightgown." Mother opened the closet door, and Sue pushed the red book underneath the mattress.

Then she was undressed—Mother's hands were cool— and dressed in her nightgown and slipped between the sheets. A lavender sachet was put into the pillowcase, its clean, sharp scent promoting sleep. Blinds drawn.

"Any better?" Mother whispered.

Sue nodded. It felt like a huge motion, like jumping out of the haymow. After a moment she heard the soft click of the door shutting.

The heavy smell of roasting chicken hung on the air. If she opened her eyes, Sue thought she would be able to see it, like a streak of grease. But after a time it receded, and only the scent of lavender remained.

When she awakened, it was dark outside, and Mother stood at the edge of the bed, nearly invisible in her calico print dress. Sue could smell mint tea.

"Are you awake?" Mother asked softly.

"Yes."

"I thought you might like this now." There was a light chink as Mother set the little porcelain teapot on the bedside table, and next to it one of her thin china teacups in its saucer. "Let me help you sit up." She tucked a spare pillow behind Sue's back.

Sue felt weak, and clean inside, and very light, like a leaf. It was good to hear the tea poured, to hold the china cup by its curlicued handle and touch the delicate rim to her lips. Mother sat on the edge of the bed to watch her drink. They couldn't see each other's faces.

The moment had a piercing sweetness. Mother in the shadows was a mother from a song, no longer her astringent self, but all made up of love and tenderness. Sue felt carried back to much younger days, cared for the way she had been only as a little child. Tears welled, aching, in her eyes, and slowly receded.

"That better?" Mother asked when most of the tea was gone.

"Yes," Sue said. She was aware of keeping her voice thin and weak-sounding, not to forfeit this attention.

"Clare helped me with supper and dishes," Mother said. "It's good for her to help."

Sue put cup and saucer on the unseen table with a perilous-sounding clatter. "Was Mrs. Coombs all right?" She had a queasy memory of Mother helping the old lady up the path to her front door, an unpainted house, a small neat dooryard with a wide growth of goldenrod surrounding it. The yard had once been larger, but care of it had been given up.

Mother sighed. "I wish I thought so, Susan." It was strange to hear Mother sound unsure. It made Sue feel grown up.

"What's the matter with her?"

"She has a weak heart," Mother said. "It takes twice the work to make a living on that hill as it does here in the valley. She doesn't have the strength, and poor Johnny doesn't have the mind."

The words of Father's diary flashed in Sue's mind: "Eliza Coombs there with her little boy—Tolman's wound still troubles him very much." Now Tolman was dead, and Johnny was grown, taking care of her himself, dragging her over the buggy wheel and ripping her skirt.

"What will become of them?"

"I don't know," Mother said with a sharp sigh. "If the Lord's going to provide, He'd better snap to it! There, it's Sunday, and I've said something I shouldn't. I'm going to bed before the day's a total loss."

51

9

When Sue awakened, the sun was high, and breakfast sounds had begun: the coffee grinder and, out in the yard, Mother's voice. Clare must be helping.

It's good for her to help. Sue burrowed into the pillow. Her nausea was gone, but she felt achy and thinned out somehow. She had dreamed all night: marching soldiers, a red calf in the grass. When she dozed, the soldiers marched straight up to the calf; fear that they would trample it snapped her eyes wide open. Then a barn was burning, the calf bawled—

She awoke again with a jolt. Mother was at the door, her face not dim, half seen and tender, but sharp, full of the day's cares. She evaluated Sue the way Father looked the horses over in the morning.

"A day in bed won't do you a bit of harm."

Sue raised up on her elbows, about to protest. It was Monday, washday. Already the water would be heating in the boiler.

"No," Mother said, "stay right where you are! If you feel like eating, Clare will bring you breakfast."

When Clare came in, it felt like yesterday's double vision. A flushed face, slightly resentful, shoulders squared against the load: That was usually Sue's own face, glimpsed in the mirror above Clare's bureau. With a start that seemed to jolt her stomach Sue saw Clare's white hands place the tray on the bedside table, her own brown hands reach out for the tea and dark-burned toast.

"I'm sorry," she said. "The wash—"

"We'll manage," Clare said briskly—just like Mother. Play-acting, Sue thought, listening to Clare's quick steps down the stairs. Clare was always playacting.

Of course they were encouraged to playact, weren't they? Everything she'd learned about becoming a woman was a form of disguise. Mask your strength. Lower your voice. Never seem to be angry or to perspire.

Yet the work, the everlasting work. Wash, sew, cook, preserve, briskly, efficiently, and without ever complaining. All this to be accomplished by the very same person. Tie on a clean apron and take up your work. Take off the apron and pretend you don't know what the word *work* means.

This was a woman's life in Westminster West, and Father should have known that. He had a mother, who did the same things. But he had been away a long time, with men only. He must have believed that Jane Wilcox's "mild, sweet expression" told everything about her.

At noon, flushed, chin high, mouth firm, Clare came with the dinner tray. Now she's being gallant! Sue thought. But she knew how Clare felt: tired and dreading the afternoon. Washday went on and on.

All right, she thought, when Clare had taken the tray away. She didn't feel particularly sick anymore. Time to get up and help. She stood, reaching for her dress. But a wave of darkness rolled up from beneath her eyes, her knees weakened, and she found herself sitting half collapsed on the bed again.

She waited for her head to clear. Sometimes this happened when she stood up too quickly.

After a minute she pushed herself upright. At once the floorboards spun and sank. She squeezed her eyes shut. Head . . . stomach . . . Lie down. But the pillow was so far away, a long, dizzy plunge.

Slowly she lowered herself. By the time her cheek touched the pillow her whole body was shaking. She lay on her side for a long time, not daring even to turn over.

At last she rolled onto her back, inch by inch. The spirit level in her head hesitated. She could almost feel the little bubble quiver, and settle.

I *am* sick. A spinning, sinking feeling, as if her head were full of maple keys, fluttering to the ground. Don't move. Don't move.

". . . a weakness brought on by exposure to the Southern climate."

By midafternoon, when Mother came up, Sue felt a little better, but only the smallest motion was allowed. Any more and she seemed to cross a boundary into sickness. Stay here, the spirit level said. This is the balance point—this narrow range.

Mother felt her forehead, with a hand that was rough and red and smelled of soap. "No fever. Well, you do see dizziness with the grippe sometimes. I'm sure you'll feel perfectly well tomorrow."

But all night the Grand Army of the Republic passed in review before Sue's dreaming eyes. The blue legs moved in unison, ranks stretching unbroken to the horizon. The boots tramped steadily, the bayonets pricked the sky, on and on in monstrous uniformity.

10

THE NEXT MORNING Sue got herself as far as the hallway. But the ranks of stairs were like the soldiers' legs. They set off the spinning, and she turned back, leaning on the wall, and lay down again. "I'm sending for Dr. Melton!" Mother said.

After breakfast Father came upstairs. "Susie! Not like *you* to be sick!"

"And ironing day." Sue could smell the flatirons heating and hear the brisk clip-clop as Ed rode away on Bright.

"Clare's helping," Father said with a hint of pride.

"Oh, good!" Sue heard herself say, quick as a knife. "Every girl should learn how to iron!"

Father drew his mouth down to keep himself from smiling. Sue felt her face go red. She hadn't meant to say that. It had said itself. The mean, quick-witted person who lived inside her said these things, quicker than she could think of them.

"Still full of vinegar, anyway," Father said, almost admiringly. He stood turning his straw hat between his hands. He'd been up and working two hours already, had his breakfast, and now onward, in the perpetual rush to keep up with summer. He had taken this minute out, but what to do with it? "Get better now, all right?"

Sue's heart thudded suddenly, so hard she thought he might hear it. They were alone together. The diary was under the mattress, just below her hand and hip. Could she bring it out? Could she possibly just . . . show it to him? Say, "I found this"? Wait for what he said next?

Shockingly the vision of his white legs, his dark curling hair passed before her mind's eye. She felt herself blush.

"Well, Susie, got to make hay while the sun shines." His smile deepened the creases beside his eyes. So many smiles, so many long hours squinting under a straw hat, forking the hay and driving the horses across the vast green hill, so many years. Maybe he really had forgotten. How could she remind him? "A man's head . . ."

"Okay," she started to say. But he was already gone; his footsteps were halfway down the stairs.

That was like Father, always just out of reach. The kitchen door closed, the horses' big hooves thudded slowly in the yard, and the mowing machine wheels rumbled. Sue felt a sudden surge of loneliness. She reached under the mattress for the red book and lay with her fingers lightly touching its spine.

For a long time the house was still. The smell of hot iron and hot cloth, tinged with starch and blueing, drifted in the window, and the sound of voices. Clare. Clare talking with Mother, Clare being reminded to lick her finger and touch it lightly to the flatiron to test its heat. Clare, who before this did only the daintiest of pressing. Clare should learn to iron—that was true. So there was some good in being sick.

After a while buggy wheels and hoofbeats, Ed's voice in the yard, sounding light, cheerful, and false. Sue thought, Ed doesn't like the new doctor. Ed didn't realize how often his eloquent voice gave him away, or else he didn't care.

It was hard to see what Ed objected to, though. Dr. Melton was young and round-eyed and very serious, but his voice was kind, and he managed to conduct a thorough examination without making the process seem immodest. He was interested in the nausea; he probed her head with his fingertips; he looked inside her ears and asked after other symptoms. But all Sue had to report was dizziness.

At last Dr. Melton sat down in the rocking chair, looking thoughtful. He was sweating. Mother stepped to the door and called for Clare to bring a pitcher of ice water.

"Well, Mrs. Gorham," he said after a refreshing sip, "I find no organic cause for your daughter's malady."

Mother was pouring for Sue. The stream of water jerked and missed the glass for a second, slopping onto the bedclothes. "No—no possibility of consumption?"

A coldness spread down Sue's back at the word, and Clare sat down on the bed, as if her knees had suddenly loosened.

"No," Dr. Melton said firmly. "There's no reason to suppose anything of the kind. But that doesn't mean there is no cause for concern. Thousands of young women take to their beds each year with similar complaints and many never resume a normal life."

Mother's eyes widened. "Are you suggesting—"

"Nerves," Dr. Melton said simply. "As a girl's body becomes ready to accept woman's role, her system becomes more susceptible to the stresses of modern life—"

"Dr. Melton"—Mother interrupted impatiently—"this is Westminster West. We don't live a very modern life. Are you sure it isn't just a touch of the sun?"

Sue jumped. ". . . a weakness brought on by exposure to the Southern climate."

"It's possible that the heat of the past few days may have overstressed a delicately balanced system," Dr. Melton said,

57

a little defensively. Suddenly the bed trembled. Sue glanced up. Clare had turned her face away from Dr. Melton, and she was laughing. Sue pressed her lips thin and flat to hold back her own smile.

"I must stress the importance of rest. A light, airy room like this one, dainty, nourishing foods, such as fruits and junkets, and plenty of quiet, to allow the nerves time to recover."

"Very well."

Dr. Melton frowned at the novel on the bedside table.

"Not so much reading," he said. "In woman the heart must predominate, not the head. Excessive reading can cause mental imbalance. Those poor girls who are entering colleges now will pay a terrible price. But, Mrs. Gorham, with care and good nursing this vertigo should pass."

"Well, thank you for your advice," Mother said, escorting him out of the room. She closed the door behind him, but Sue and Clare waited to hear footsteps going down the stairs before daring to laugh out loud.

"Oh, Clary! Did you ever hear anything so ridiculous?"

" 'A delicately balanced system!' I nearly said, 'Do you mean *Sue?*' "

Something in Clare's words was hurtful, but it didn't matter. For the moment they were as close as they'd ever been. "Doesn't he know?" Sue said. "Farm girls don't *have* nerves. It must have been the sun."

"You were out picking currants for a long time," Clare said hopefully. It was a comfort to be able to sense Clare's thoughts. Sue had spent her whole life misunderstanding Father and Mother, but Clare she did know.

"I'm going to get up," she said, putting her water glass on the tray. Dr. Melton had made the whole thing seem silly, but also a little dangerous, as if merely by feeling faint, she had joined the permanent sisterhood of invalids. She pushed back the covers and stood.

"Susie!"

"Thought you had a little more sense!"

She was back on the pillows, and Mother's face, Clare's face were near and anxious. "Are you all right?" Clare asked.

"I thought . . . he was so silly. I thought . . . Did I fall?"

"Mostly on the bed," Mother said, tucking the sheet firmly around Sue's shoulders. "Maybe he wasn't as silly as he sounded, but I'm bound to say, I don't know what could have happened to upset your nerves!"

"Nothing! Nothing's happened!" Sue felt herself starting to cry. "It's *stupid!* I'm *not* sick!"

"Of course not. Just rest, dear. Close your eyes." Mother's hand was on Sue's brow, and the cool pressure weighted her eyelids, pushed her down into sleep.

11

THAT SLEEP LASTED for days. Sue lay still, her head pressing a narrow dent in the pillow. Much of the time she seemed to dream, but nothing was clear even then—a sense of sharp tossing horns, sometimes, or a high and heavy thing looming over her.

She must have eaten, she must have used the chamber pot, but afterward she couldn't remember that. She only remembered opening her eyes to see Mother at the bedside watching intently, Ed reading a book, Clare rubbing cucumber cream into her reddened hands. Voices: Dr. Melton, Dr. Campbell, Reverend Stevens. "No, nothing hurts," she remembered saying to someone, and it was true. But the world seemed too bright and complex to look at. She wanted to dive deep into sleep, which seemed to contain some knowledge or nourishment she needed.

After a few days Mother said, "I'm afraid they know and won't tell me. I'm afraid it *is* consumption!"

"Nonsense, Janey!" Aunt Mary Braley. They sounded as if they were at the doorway. "Dr. Campbell would tell you. He's got no more tact than a *turtle*, that man!"

A little choked laugh from Mother. "Aunt Mary! Oh, I'm sorry. I haven't got my mother anymore. I've got to cry to *someone*. But I don't understand this business of nerves. That's for rich city women, isn't it?"

Mother's voice, Aunt Mary's voice were like thoughts in Sue's head. Without opening her eyes, she could see the two of them: a big dark bulk for Aunt Mary and Mother little, wiry, and quick.

"Well now, Janey, we're more like city women here in Westminster West than we used to be, don't you think? Seems to me we're awful genteel. Rhoda Ranney could lift up a barrel of cider and drink from the bung. We've declined considerable since those days."

"Perhaps we've gained in other ways," Mother suggested.

"No, Jane, I don't think you've gained s'very much. You've got all the work we ever had, and you've got to keep your hands nice, too! Be all right if you had two bodies. You could work one and keep the other ready for company! But I've yet to meet the woman who could manage that. It's no wonder the young girls are afraid to try! But there! You said you missed your mother, and I've given you a scold. That's motherly, ain't it? Go and get done what you need to. I'll set and watch Sue awhile."

Sue lay listening to the humph and rustle of Aunt Mary settling her bulk in the chair. After a moment the old woman asked quietly, "You awake, Susie?"

Sue opened her eyes.

"Want I should read to you? I brought a book, but I can't seem to read to myself. Spent so many years readin' while I churned, it's hard for me to get the good of a book settin' still. I miss the cream sloshin'—used to think I was like some old sailor missin' the waves!"

A pause. Aunt Mary sighed largely. "Well, my tongue does run away with me, and that's a fact! I'll just set and keep still if I can."

Sue realized she hadn't answered. "No . . . tell me a story."

61

Aunt Mary laughed. "If that ain't just like a child! What would you like to hear?"

"Tell me . . . about wartimes."

Aunt Mary's bulk seemed to become stiller. "Now why do you want to hear about misfortunes, and you layin' there?"

Sue didn't answer.

Aunt Mary sighed again. "Well, like cures like, they say. My war stories are just sickness and sorrow. I nursed awhile at the hospital in Brattleboro, on the old mustering ground. Where the fairground is now."

"Yes."

"A good many of us feel they might have chosen a different spot to hold the fairs," Aunt Mary said. "I never go but what I start to sorrowin' over somebody—like as not poor Johnny Coombs."

"Johnny Coombs?"

"Why, didn't you ever hear this story? That camp was halfway a hospital as soon as ever it was set up. Hundreds of fellows never got any farther south than that. Took sick and died, all cramped in there together with one another's coughs and fevers. Poor Eliza took Johnny—just a little boy—to see his father off, and he came back with some fever. When he got through it, he was the way he is now."

"Oh. I didn't know that."

"Course, Eliza never should have taken him. She feels it yet. All the child they were ever going to have." Aunt Mary sighed. "Well, nobody can say Johnny hasn't been a good son within his limits, but his gauge is set pretty narrow."

Sue let her eyes close, seeing the camp, a little bright-eyed boy holding his mother's hand.

* * *

62

Later. Aunt Mary was knitting, and Delyra Goodhue was at the door, small and slight in her black cashmere dress. "Hello, Mary. I came over to see if I could spell Jane for a while—might have known I'd find you here!"

"Shh." The chair creaked sharply as Aunt Mary got up and moved to the doorway. "She's sleepin' again. Now, Delyra, there's no need for you to tax yourself. I can set here all day if I'm a mind to—can't be late to dinner, 'cause there isn't any till I make it!"

"Oh, I can *sit* as well as anyone!" Delyra Goodhue said, with a little laugh. "Be a rest for me. Homer and I finished with our currant jelly this morning, and I'm a little worn." Though their voices were lowered, they were perfectly distinct, and Sue closed her eyes again.

"You're well enough for jelly makin', then?"

"Homer does a good deal of it. I sort and stem, and he does the stirring and squeezing. He does take hold—as good as having another woman in the house!"

"A nice man without notions is as good as a woman any day!" Aunt Mary said stoutly, and laughed. "There! That's broad-minded for you!"

"How is Susan, do you think?"

"I don't call her *real* sick. You know, I've seen a lot of sickness in the family lately, Delyra, and there's a look to it. Sue's out of frame some way, no doubt about it, but she don't need watchin'. I wouldn't stay, except I know how Jane can be." Sue's eyes almost opened at this.

Delyra Goodhue said. "Jane's seen trouble."

"Then she ought to know this isn't it! But there! It clears the sight of some and clouds the sight of others. I knew she'd be in a fret and not gettin' work done, so I came."

"Clare's helping in the kitchen, I see."

63

"Yes, I was glad to see her there. I like Clare 'most as well as Susie, but Janey's spoiled her terrible, imaginin' she's delicate—"

"Clare was sickly."

"Clare was *sick, once!* Jane should have put her to work once she was better, for the sake of her character, if nothin' else. I declare, lookin' at the work *you* do—and you *are* sick— I should be ashamed to raise a girl like Clare!"

"If we had nursed a cousin and seen her die when we were girls, Mary, maybe we'd think differently."

Nursed a cousin? Who? Cousin Caroline and Cousin Charles both died just as the war began. Had *Mother* nursed Caroline?

Aunt Mary was silent for a moment. Then she said, in a voice that trembled slightly, "I used to worry about poor Laura, after she'd had to watch her sister die, and I planned out how I was goin' to help ease her mind, and now there's no need for it and no time. . . . I *will* leave then, Delyra. Seems as if I've got to be out in the air when these thoughts come upon me."

She left and Delyra Goodhue sat by the bed straight and still as if she had found a perfect resting point between her strength and her weakness. She gave off a faint scent of peppermint.

Why had *Mother* nursed Cousin Caroline? She would have been just a girl herself. The fading old daguerreotype on Mother's bureau, the brown lock of hair in the frame, and the little scrap of paper: "for my Cousin and Dearest Friend, Jane Wilcox." But no one had ever said what those things meant. Sue opened her eyes, but more time must have passed than she'd thought. The chair beside the bed was empty.

"I don't see why a hardworking country girl shouldn't enjoy a fit of the vapors just as much as a society belle!" Dr. Campbell's voice. Cool hands had partially awakened her. "She'll get over it in her own good time."

Mother said nothing. She's angry, Sue thought, and later Mother said, ". . . doctors don't know a thing!"

"A Boston specialist?" someone suggested. Aunt Emma? Something in that thought stirred Sue to open her eyes. Mother and Aunt Emma were watching her.

Then they were gone, and Minnie was whispering, "Wake up, Susie! Listen! The school burned down!"

"What?" Sue's voice came thick and husky. She had not used it in a long time. "Which school?"

"Ours, last night! They say lightning, but there was no storm! It's the firebug! It has to be!"

Everything was jumbled together in Sue's head. After a minute she said, "Henry must be so pleased."

"Pleased?" Minnie's face was close, her eyes as big and shiny as marbles.

"He's been saying—"

"Oh, your mother's coming! Don't say I told you. I wasn't supposed to get you excited."

Sue almost smiled at that. Did she really seem excited?

Minnie said, "I'm on my way home—day off. Johnny Coombs is driving me."

Sue managed to raise her eyebrows. That was response enough for Minnie. She groaned. "Yes! Susie, he likes me!"

Then Mother was at the door. "Minnie, Johnny seems impatient." Sue heard Minnie's quick steps down the stairs. Mother came to the bed, rested her hand on Sue's brow, and

Sue closed her eyes. But I don't know anything about the school, she thought, and something seemed to gather together in her mind, like a horse getting ready to stand.

The next day Clare brought a bowl of raspberries. They were red as rubies in the green china dish. Clare's dress smelled like sunshine, and the raspberries smelled like roses.

Sue pushed herself up a little on the pillow. It seemed to take a great effort. "What day is it?"

"July twenty-seventh."

July twenty-seventh? That was more than a week . . . "Have I been—what have I been doing?"

"Don't you *remember*?" Clare asked in a fascinated voice.

"Oh. Yes." But it didn't seem possible that so much time had passed, and Sue had wondered for a moment if she'd been out of her head, raving.

She looked at Clare. How strange—Clare was red-faced, sweaty, tired. Delicate, fragile Clare, who must not overdo. Work didn't make her look fragile, though. It made her look sturdy. Clare must hate that.

"When are you going away?" she asked. "Isn't it soon?"

Clare flushed. "I can't go with you like this!"

No. No, she probably couldn't. Sue took a raspberry from the green dish, crushed it against the roof of her mouth. The sweet, warm fragrance flooded her senses. Clare, out in the hot sun picking raspberries? What had come over Mother?

"Clare?" Mother called from the foot of the stairs.

"Come up!" Clare answered. "She's awake!"

12

LIFE DID NOT CHANGE overnight. Sue still slept a great deal. She was still dizzy. But the light had come on again inside her head.

Mother and Clare carried up all the work they could. Perhaps they'd been doing that right along, and Sue hadn't noticed. Now she felt the whole weight of Mother's anxious attention, her eyes glancing up from sewing or sorting, the intense listening when eyes and hands were occupied.

Often Sue felt a pleased little smile on her lips in response, which she quickly smoothed out. But other times the worry in Mother's face seemed to light dry tinder inside Sue. She would notice how thin her own hands looked, how pale, and how far away they seemed from her head on its pillows, and she would remember that word, *consumption*. Dr. Melton said she did *not* have it. Everyone said she did not have it. But the fear in Mother's eyes said "maybe."

"Rest!" Mother would say if Sue reached for a bean to snap or a sheet to hem. "It's so easy to work yourself into a relapse."

After a few days Clare began to make a little sound when Mother said this. Probably only Sue could hear it because Mother never turned her head. Sue realized: *Clare* doesn't think I'm truly sick.

Clare should know!

It was time to dry the lavender. Mother and Clare filled their aprons with blue spikes and brought them up to spill across Sue's bed. With plain white yarn they tied the spikes together, a few at a time. The air was full of the cool, clean fragrance.

Suddenly Clare broke the silence. The quick inbreath before she spoke told Sue she'd been struggling to make herself speak. "Mother, couldn't Sue go to the mountains in my place?"

Clare didn't mean it. She was really asking, Am *I* still going? But Sue's heart thudded twice. Mother's hands stilled, and she looked sharply at Clare, meditating some response. The sound of buggy wheels interrupted.

"That will be your aunt Emma," Mother said. She stood as she spoke, stripped off collar and cuffs, reached back to untie her long apron. By the time she reached the front door, her fresh, starched cuffs would be in place and her hair would be smooth.

Clare bent lower over the lavender. Sue could see the side of her face, flushed and sullen. After a minute she said, "I do think *one* of us should go!" Jerkily her fingers went on picking up the lavender. "You don't believe me, but—I'd be *happy* if you went."

Sue couldn't help smiling. "No, you wouldn't! You'd only try to be."

Clare laughed shakily, and tears spilled down her cheeks. "It wouldn't work! I'd *hate* you! But *could* you go, Sue? Are you well enough?"

No, Sue thought. She hadn't challenged the spirit level in the past few days. She kept her head propped, even when she slid over the edge of the bed to use the chamber pot.

But she knew what the level wanted. Stay here. Lie still. It was clearer than the Voice of Conscience, for which she'd been taught to listen since early childhood.

"I can't!" she said, tears starting in her own eyes.

"But you *are* a little better?"

"Yes, I'm a little better."

Clare nodded decisively. "Then I'm going! There has to be a way. Why is Aunt Emma here, anyway? Why haven't they come up?" There was a low murmur of voices from the dooryard, no words clear. Clare strained to hear, and Sue noticed the stubborn set of her chin, remembered Mother saying—a long time ago, when they were little—"That child has the disposition of a mule!" For years now they had been ignoring that strength, but Clare still had it.

"How can you, Clary?" she asked. "What will Mother do for help?"

Clare's face crumpled. "I don't *know!* Oh, Susie! All that washing! All those pies! You always made it look easy! Even when you were thirteen, you were so good at everything! When you got sick, I thought *I'd* be the good one, but I didn't think it would be so long. Susie, I don't *want* to anymore!"

Does she think if she cries hard enough, I'll just stop being dizzy? Sue wondered. When *she* had cried, when Clare was sick, had she thought crying would help? No, she had cried alone and washed the tears away with cold water so no one would know.

And when the work was too much, she had tried even harder and smiled pridefully. Suddenly she had an image of a boy standing before a laden oxcart. The oxen tossed their horns sullenly, took a step, and the boy glanced proudly at his father—who *needed* him!—and never moved.

Never moved again.

Mother had needed her, too, and she had stood stubbornly in front of that crushing load, proved herself reliable, and Mother kept on needing her. Now Mother needed Clare, and Clare was crying!

"I'm sorry," she said stiffly.

"It's not your fault. But it isn't *fair!* I've been looking forward to this trip for so long!"

No, it isn't fair, Sue thought, with such a powerful mix of pity and anger that she thought her heart might crack. It wasn't fair for Clare to be asked twice, and Sue never. It wasn't fair for Clare to be disappointed.

Nothing's fair. There's no such thing as fair. She wanted to put her arms around Clare's neck and cry along with her because each of them was stuck in her own life. Clare must be Clare, and Sue must be Sue, and neither of them could go to the White Mountains.

Now she could hear Mother and Aunt Emma talking their way slowly through the house and up the stairs. "Better splash your face," she said to Clare, who seemed suddenly far away—still on the edge of the bed but very far away.

Clare went quickly to the washstand and came back to the bed and the lavender. Mother and Aunt Emma came in. Aunt Emma's skirts made a stiff, expensive sound, and her face had the rested look that Sue always thought of as the true expression of wealth.

"Clare," Mother said.

Reluctantly Clare turned to face them.

"You've been such a help, and I felt sorry that you might not have your fun. But Emma has suggested that Minnie come here to help me, so you can get away."

The back of Clare's neck went red. "Oh, Aunt Emma! Mother!" She hugged them both, and Sue watched. Yes, she thought. This was the way things *would* happen.

*　*　*

The next few days passed in a frenzy of dressmaking. Even Sue was allowed to sew on trim and to set the hem on a skirt. It was good to be at work again. The hum of the sewing machine treadle downstairs seemed to set her thoughts free.

This trip would put things right again, she decided. Clare had learned to work. When she came back, Sue would be recovering, and they would share the tasks, side by side like Bright and Lucky in double harness. Perhaps this winter Aunt Emma would invite Sue to Boston for a visit. Perhaps next summer *she* would be the one to go to the mountains.

The last morning Clare brought Sue's oatmeal, and a little later she hurried in again, wearing her handsome green traveling dress. Her eyes were bright, her whole face was bright and alive. Clare is beautiful, Sue thought.

Clare stooped and kissed her cheek. "Keep on getting better, Susie! I'll see you in three weeks!"

The buggy rattled away. An hour later Mother came back with Minnie.

13

THE KITCHEN DOOR BANGED. Quick steps went all the way to Clare's back bedroom. A thump, a pause, and then Minnie was running up the stairs. She bounced into the room and kissed Sue on the cheek. "Susie! We're going to have so much fun!"

Then downstairs again, where Mother was trying to hurry the baking along. Sue was alone, but the house was full of laughter.

At dinnertime Minnie brought the tray. "Your mother says I can eat with you." She propped Sue up briskly like someone plumping a pillow.

"I'm flattered you'd want to," Sue said, "when you could sit at the table with the boys."

"I'm on vacation from boys," Minnie said, helping herself to a hot biscuit. "Remember I told you? Johnny Coombs has taken a shine to me."

"*Really?*"

"Oh, yes! And working on that barn for the Campbells, he's got an excuse to stop by at least once a day. That's why I put the idea in Mrs. Campbell's head that she could loan me to your mother."

"I thought it was Aunt Emma's idea."

"It almost was," Minnie said. "She caught on awful quick! But how are you, Susie? Feeling a lot better?"

"Y-es," Sue said cautiously.

"Good! Now if only you were downstairs, we could talk all the time. You should have that room they put me in."

"That's Clare's room," Sue said quickly. It was pretty but narrow and small and tucked away at the back of the house. "If I was going to be downstairs, I'd just as soon be in the parlor."

Mother came in just then, with her usual swift, sober glance at Sue's face. Minnie turned to her with a bounce that rocked the bed. "Mrs. Gorham! Why don't we bring Susie downstairs and put her on the couch? She must be lonely up here, and it'll save us wearing our legs out on the stairs."

Mother's eyes widened. "Well, I'm not sure. Sue needs rest and quiet—"

Father was with her, though, and his face brightened. "That's a good notion. Jane, don't you think Susie got about all the rest she needs, sleeping for a week?"

Mother said, "I guess there's no harm in trying it, just for the afternoon. No, David, you can't just take her down! I have to get things ready."

Mother and Minnie bustled upstairs and down, getting sheets and pillows, a screen, the chamber pot. Sue lay waiting. She felt nervous, and that seemed absurd. She was just going downstairs, for heaven's sake!

When all was ready, Father scooped her up and she put her arms around his neck. His shoulders were hard, as if made of wood. He smelled of sweat and the outdoors; he was warm. . . . The stairs. They were at the top of the stairs.

Sue squeezed her eyes shut. She felt a lurching downward, the strain in Father's body, and she heard a faint worried sound from Mother. Then everything became black and blurry. . . .

73

A pillow was under her head, and someone was asking a question. "Just let me be quiet," Sue murmured.

Slowly, slowly the falling leaves in her head all landed. She opened her eyes. Minnie was dusting the blue glass bowl on the mantel. She flicked the feather duster over it skillfully, carefully, and only when she was finished did she turn for an anxious look at Sue. "Oh! Are you all right?"

"I think so." The parlor, with its carpet, chairs, ornaments, and whatnots, seemed full and complex. Sue felt a moment's longing for her upstairs room, bare as a nun's cell, with the red book for a Bible—the book! With Sue out of the bed, Mother would want to turn the mattress, and she would find it.

"Minnie. Come here?" Minnie came closer. "Under my mattress there's a diary." Curiosity flared in Minnie's eyes. "Would you hide it in my closet? And if you *dare* look—"

Minnie grinned impishly. "Susie! Would I do a thing like that?" She ran upstairs. When she came back, she had Sue's small knitting basket, the needles stuck into the ball of yarn and the sleeve of a blue jersey hanging from them. She put the knitting by the sofa, within easy reach. As she bent down, she whispered, "In your boot!"

As the afternoon advanced, Sue couldn't imagine going back to her room. It was such a pleasure simply to watch Minnie dust the parlor and to see Mother a dozen times within an hour: to see Mother by random chance, to see Mother when she was thinking of something besides Sue's illness.

After supper everyone gathered: Ed at the piano, Henry with *The Agriculturalist*, while Father, spectacles astride his nose, went over some town accounts. Minnie and Sue played cribbage, but as Father closed his books, Minnie suddenly asked, "Mr. Gorham? Do the selectmen know yet if the schoolhouse fire was set?"

Father looked over his spectacles, and Mother shot a worried glance at Sue, as if expecting to see her fall to the floor in a fit of hysterics. Henry's eyes brightened.

"The selectmen won't say," he told her. "But it can't be anything else. Lightning doesn't strike out of a clear blue sky!"

Father looked for a moment as if he disagreed, as if he had seen lightning act that way, as if disaster should never be unexpected. It was the briefest expression. Sue thought maybe she imagined it. He said only, "We don't have proof either way."

"When you've had three fires *set*, you don't call the fourth an accident unless you have proof otherwise," Henry said.

"I don't see that the school fits the pattern," Ed said. "The others were barn fires, and the barns belonged to prosperous people—"

"That's what I told Papa," Minnie said. "He's just too poor to be of any interest to this fellow!"

"Could you say the Drislanes are prosperous?" Sue asked, with a strong sense of excitement and pleasure. Something had broken open; they were talking beyond the limits Mother usually set.

"I don't know why not," Minnie said. "Looks like a pretty comfortable place to me. If we went to Catholic church and saw them in their Sunday best, we'd probably know how prosperous they are!"

"Pat Drislane's a good farmer," Father said. "They do all right."

"But what about the school?" Sue asked. "That belongs to everybody, rich or poor."

"You can say that," Minnie said. "Or you can look at the

75

people concerned with running it, and they're the same ones who run everything and have the good farms."

A little silence fell in the parlor. Sue looked from Henry's brooding face to Ed's, full of mischievous awareness, to Mother's.

"Oh, I'm sorry!" Minnie said. "I didn't mean—"

"If the boot fits, wear it!" Ed said, and Henry looked up seriously.

"Minnie's right. The school is part of it."

But the school was so close, only a few hundred yards from the end of their field. If they had known it was burning, they could have seen it. The Drislanes' farm was a quarter mile up the hill, the Campbells' a half mile down . . .

"Ed," Mother said, "play another song."

After the lamps were blown out, Minnie said from the next room, "Susie? Are you asleep yet?"

"No."

"I shouldn't have said anything," Minnie said.

"What? About the fires? That's all right."

"Your mother didn't like it. You're supposed to have rest and quiet."

"I've had about all the rest and quiet I can stand," Sue said.

Minnie laughed, and the bed in the next room jounced. "This is nice, isn't it? Laying here talking?"

"Yes," Sue said, stretching on the couch. "Yes, this is nice."

14

THE NEXT MORNING Sue awakened at five-thirty, as Minnie tried to slip silently through the room. She lay through the gray dawn, listening. Father and the boys went out to the barn. The cows came in. The merinos baaed imperiously. Bright nickered, and with the three other horses was brought in from the night pasture and given oats.

Someone split kindling for the stove. I like splitting kindling, Sue thought, and she wondered if Clare had learned to do that chore. After a while breakfast smells drifted into the front parlor, and she began to feel hungry. It seemed to take forever for chores to be finished and the milk brought in and finally for Minnie to come with the tray.

"Oh! You're awake!"

"Yes." Sue lay against the pillow, waiting for the tray to be placed on her stomach.

"Don't you want to sit up?" Minnie asked. "I don't see how a person can swallow oatmeal laying down. Here." She put the tray on a chair, and before Sue knew what was happening, she was being propped upright, her feet actually over the edge of the sofa, actually touching the floor. There was nothing to rest her head against. Her neck had to stiffen and bear the whole weight by itself. For a moment it felt too weak. She had to will her muscles to tighten and make her neck into the strong column it had always been.

"There!" Minnie said. "I'll just tuck a shawl around you and run get my own tray."

Sue sat there alone. The bowl of oatmeal steamed before her.

In a moment Minnie was back, Mother behind her.

"Sue! Sitting up?"

"I was afraid she'd choke on her oatmeal," Minnie said. "I know I would if I ate laying down."

"I wish you'd support your head," Mother said. "I'm still afraid you've injured your spine."

"I don't think so," Sue murmured. Without her pillows she felt like a flower on a long, weak stem, in danger of collapsing in the middle. But if she collapsed, Minnie would be blamed. Very carefully she reached for the tray and brought a spoonful of oatmeal to her mouth, keeping her head perfectly still. Nothing happened. The spirit level did not register a tilt, and the oatmeal was hot and sweet with maple sugar.

"Don't sit up long," Mother said. "I don't want you to overdo it the first time."

"The first time?" Minnie said. "Oh, I didn't realize—"

"It's all right," Sue said. She finished her whole breakfast sitting up, and she sat up again for lunch and supper.

With Minnie there, Sue felt like a vacationer. After breakfast the house emptied, and she read or knitted, listening to sounds of work from the kitchen. Then dinner. The best fruits and berries were saved for Sue, as if she were a cherished guest. A nap, a game of cards, a cup of tea and a chat with Minnie, then supper.

Evenings they had music, gossip, and stories, with a cast of characters that spanned a century. Westminster West had long been tamed, but under Minnie's influence wolves and bears rampaged again. The Yorkers marched through to confrontation at the courthouse. Mills and taverns sprang up at the corner of the West road, flourished, faded, and sank into their cellar holes.

One evening midway through Minnie's stay Father and Henry went to a meeting about rebuilding the school. Ed stayed home to play the piano, and Minnie turned pages for him.

He finished his sonata, and leaned back with his head on one side to give her a killingly sentimental look. Then he dropped into the old war tune "When Johnny Comes Marching Home," playing softly and sweetly, settling his breath to sing.

But as the stanza ended, Minnie suddenly turned from the piano. "Mrs. Gorham, what was it *really* like when they came home?"

Sue's needle stabbed into her finger. Mother's knitting slowly sank toward her lap. Ed smiled to himself and sang very softly,

> "The village lads and lassies say,
> With roses they will strew the way,
> And we'll all
>   feel
>   gay
>   when
>   Johnny comes marching home."

After a long moment Mother said, "Well, I don't remember strewing any roses."

Minnie persisted. "But was it like the song? Was the whole town happy?"

Mother was about to turn the question aside; Sue could see it in her face. But Minnie went on. "I've always thought it must have been the most *joyful* time."

If that had been true, Mother would have said nothing. But the chance to correct a mistake was irresistible. "It was hard to be joyful. Too many didn't come home, and they surely didn't march, not all of them. Poor Otis Buxton was at death's door nearly a year. Tolman Coombs was hurt and came home to a son who would never be right—"

"But *you* must have been joyful," Minnie said. She sat down with her own knitting, but she hardly needed to glance at it. She watched Mother hopefully. The muted piano underlay the silence. Sue barely breathed, waiting.

"I remember . . . how brown he was," Mother said at last. "And thin. You wouldn't think a Vermont farm boy could *get* any leaner, but all that marching just whittled them down." After a pause she added, "He'd barely been inside a house in four years. I remember his eyes looked very pale and wild."

"Did you get married as soon as he came back?"

Slowly Mother's needles began to click again. "Soon afterward," she said, and Sue let her breath out. Of course Mother would not tell the real story. That was meant to be forgotten. For a minute or two the only sound was the soft piano notes.

Then Mother said, "They'd 'seen the elephant.' That's what they said. They hardly knew how to talk to anyone who wasn't there. And they couldn't imagine that we'd seen a few elephants, too."

"What do you think I am?" For the first time Sue put herself on Mother's side of the garden gate. She had seen her dearest friend die. Did that compare with going to war? I don't know, Sue thought.

Mother's face wore its usual calm, authoritative expression. Behind that what was she remembering? Those well-known public events—the war, the deaths—had this shadowy private dimension that Sue had never suspected and that affected everything. A shiver ran down her back, and she wrapped the afghan more closely around her.

15

Toward the end of the second week Minnie picked blackberries, and the next morning she and Mother sat on the step sorting them.

The big front door was open. From the couch Sue could just see the side of Minnie's face, and her hands, red and black from the juice.

"I could sort some," she called.

"Not on my good sofa and my good carpet, you couldn't!" Mother called back gaily. It was that kind of morning, crisp and cool, with a brilliant white, clear light over everything.

As Mother turned back to the berries, Sue saw behind her the shifting green leaves of the maple and the bright sky showing through. A swallow dived. The gray cat arched herself against Minnie's side. I want to be out there, Sue thought.

Without even thinking about it, she stood up. Clare's white afghan fell around her feet. She stepped over it.

Minnie looked up. *"Susie!"*

Sue took another step. Her legs felt weak, as if her bones had turned to water. Her knees were going to fold. . . .

Mother's form filled the bright doorway and blackened it. An arm around her waist, helping—

No. Helping her onto the sofa again.

"Susan Gorham, what on earth do you think you're doing? You can hardly sit up, let alone walk!" Mother pressed her against the sofa's back, and Sue laughed weakly as her strength collapsed before Mother's.

"Now for goodness sake, stay there! If you want to sort berries that badly, we'll put newspaper down on the carpet and let you!"

"Don't you think—" Minnie began in a troubled voice, but she didn't go on.

"Does your Mother *want* you to be an invalid?"

In the dark, from their beds, Minnie and Sue could say anything to each other. Nonetheless, Sue felt an inner squirm at this. "Of course not. She wants me to get well."

"She put you back on that sofa quick enough!"

"She was *worried!*"

"I'm worried, too, but I'd have walked you out to the step if you were my child."

"*Minnie!*"

"Maybe she likes having someone to nurse," Minnie said. "It's enough to make me want to be sick, the way she takes care of you."

"I don't know what else she could do!"

"Make it harder," Minnie said promptly. "Be cross. That's what my mother would do, God bless her!"

With difficulty Sue smoothed the irritation out of her voice. "Minnie, Mother—Mother had to nurse her own cousin until she died, when she was only a little older than we are. It makes her worry more when one of us is sick—"

"So *that's* why she lets Clare lay around the way she does!" Minnie said, on a note of triumph. "I always wondered—"

"*Lie* around!" Sue said sharply. "Not lay, *lie!*" She wanted to defeat the avid, curious note in Minnie's voice. If Minnie brought gossip in, she could take gossip away.

There was a long pause. Then Minnie said, "If my grammar isn't good enough for you, Sue Gorham, I don't have to speak at all!"

Neither of them spoke for a few minutes. Finally Sue said, "This is stupid!"

"Is it? But you don't think it's stupid to *lie* on your couch and let your mother pretend you're sick!"

"I *was* sick!"

"But you're better! Aren't you? Don't you think you should be getting up and walking? If she won't let you—*hey!*" The anger dropped out of Minnie's voice, replaced by excitement. "Why don't you get up now? I'll help! You can practice at night till you're steady on your feet, and then you can show her—"

"I'm going to sleep," Sue said, hunching her shoulder and pushing her head into the pillow.

"Oh, come on, Sue! Don't go to bed mad!"

"I'm not mad," Sue muttered. "I'm *angry!*" She heard a quick, sharp breath from the other room, and then nothing more.

The next day was Sunday, and Sue awakened late. Minnie had gone through the parlor in complete silence. At breakfast time she brought in only one tray. A moment later Sue heard her in the kitchen. "I'll eat out here this morning, Mrs. Gorham."

That brought Mother in a few minutes later. "Susan, is there some trouble between you and Minnie?"

Sue felt herself blush. "No, I—I have a little headache."

Instantly she wished she hadn't said it. Mother felt her brow, brought chamomile tea, insisted she lie down, and tucked her in an extra shawl. She could hardly bring herself to leave for church until Sue professed to feel much better.

When they were gone, Minnie came in with her Bible. Sue opened her own, and they sat in silence. Sue stared at the fishhooks and squiggles that were supposed to make words. After a few minutes she realized that Minnie had not yet turned a page.

This *is* stupid, she thought. All because Minnie was right . . . almost right. "Minnie?"

Minnie stared at her Bible as if absorbed, slowly turned the page, and then looked up, with apparent reluctance. "Yes?"

Sue couldn't bring herself to apologize. Instead she said, "You could help me walk *now*. Would you?"

A slow, deep flush rose in Minnie's cheeks. She moved the red marker and closed the Bible. "All right." Sue sat up, Minnie put a strong arm around her waist, and they stood up together.

Too sudden. Sue felt the light drain out of her head, and she collapsed on the couch again.

"Slower next time," Minnie said. They rested a moment. Then slowly they rose. Sue swayed, and braced her legs, and waited. She felt as tall as Abraham Lincoln, light-headed with altitude. But she was on her feet.

"Minnie?" Her voice came in a gasp.

"What?" Minnie asked.

"Minnie, I was a pig last night. I'm sorry." She could apologize to Minnie. She could never, ever apologize to Clare.

Minnie's arm tightened around Sue's waist for a moment. "Me, too," she said. "Can you move your trotters, piggy? This is your chance to get outdoors for a minute."

Slowly, step by step, they made it to the doorstep. Sue leaned against the lintel, looking at the barns, the wrinkled merinos in the pasture, the maple with a halo of golden leaves at the top.

"You're so weak—I didn't realize." Minnie sounded worried.

"I'll get stronger," Sue said. "But make *sure* you don't tell Mother!" If her weakness worried Minnie, how much more it would trouble Mother! Sue felt protective, as if Mother were still that shocked and grieving girl.

Each night after that Sue walked, across the room, around the room, and once all the way to Minnie's bedroom. Her legs felt liquid, and having made it that far, she had to lean on the bureau. She looked into the mirror at her face, heavily shadowed in the light of the kerosene lamp. How pale she seemed. Minnie, beside her, was as dark as a Negro by comparison.

Suddenly Minnie crossed her eyes and stuck out her tongue at the mirror. Then she bent over with both hands pressed to her mouth, trying to hold back her giggles.

"Shh!" Sue hissed, gazing at the interesting hollows in her cheeks, the fevered-looking darkness of her dilated eyes. Then she stretched her mouth like a frog's and tried to make her eyes bulge, and Minnie squealed. Sue started laughing, too. After a moment they heard Mother's sleepy voice. "Girls? Is anything wrong?"

Minnie gasped and wiped her hands down her face, smoothing it out. "No, Mrs. Gorham, we're just talking. Sorry."

There was a murmur from Mother and Father's bedroom, and then Father said, "That's all right. Enjoy yourselves." His voice was indulgent, and Sue suddenly remembered: Minnie was leaving in two days. Minnie would go, and Clare would come back. A small, hard lump, like a potato, seemed to form in Sue's heart.

No, she reminded herself. Clare had learned to work. She would help Sue get back on her feet. They would begin to work in double harness. Clare would make sure that Sue was the one invited to join the next Campbell excursion. That last kiss on the cheek had promised.

But over the next two days the lump in Sue's heart grew heavier and harder.

16

THE VACATION PARTY arrived in Westminster West on Tuesday evening, and Clare rested overnight at the Campbell mansion. In the morning Mother took Minnie back and brought Clare home.

Sue waited nervously. The house was empty. The big hall door stood open to the morning sun and breezes. Once Sue found herself on her feet looking out. She had taken herself to the doorway as unconsciously as if she were perfectly well. Now her knees weakened, but she stood anyway, half leaning against the lintel, until she heard the sound of hooves. Then she returned to the sofa and lay back against the pillows.

The buggy stopped at the lawn, outside Sue's range of vision. A creak, the swish of skirts . . .

Clare came through the big door. She glanced into the parlor and started. "Sue! Down here? You're better!"

The weight on Sue's chest began to burn. Clare hadn't asked, then, and Mother hadn't told her. As clear as print Sue could read Clare's hopes. "No," she said, faintly, above the rapid thudding of her heart. "I'm not much better."

"Oh." After a moment's hesitation Clare came into the room.

There were many elegant new touches to her dress, and her hair was put up differently, in a simple, graceful sweep.

Her face was creamy pale, but her composed, distant expression was shattered. Clare was off-balance, and Sue waited. Maybe everything would still be all right. Clare could still come and give her a hug, ask how she felt with real concern, and then she would say, "I am improving. I've started to walk."

But Clare's parted lips closed and firmed again. She stood unmoving in the center of the room, saying nothing but making Sue very aware of the afghan spread over her untidily, the books on the floor, the knitting basket trailing its blue sleeve, the screen in the corner.

"My, Sue," she said after a moment, "you've certainly moved in here!"

Mother came through the front door. "Clare, why don't you rest? I'll get dinner going, and the boys will bring in your trunk when they come up from the field." She disappeared into the kitchen, and the stove lids began to rattle.

Clare sank into the rocker in a graceful, exhausted way, the old Clare, with gestures more polished and convincing.

Sue took a deep breath, hoping to throw off the pressure in her chest. "How was it?" Her voice came out thin as a thread.

"Beautiful," Clare said vaguely. "Everyone knows Aunt Emma, even though she's very country, because the Campbells are such important men."

Aunt Emma "very country"? She'd always seemed "very city" to Sue—at least, for Westminster West. "So people were nice to you?"

"Yes." Clare looked around the room and then back to the sofa. Sue felt an unspoken push. Get off! Get up! Her heart thumped, painfully.

I'm here now, she thought. And I'm not moving!

"Hi there!"

A man's voice, at the open door. A black shape against the light. Sue's head spun. She squeezed her eyes shut.

"Minnie around?"

Johnny Coombs!

"No," Clare stammered, "she's—she's gone back to the Campbells."

Sue heard his footsteps in the hall. He was *in* their house! What did he think he was doing? That door wasn't for just anyone to walk through. She opened her eyes again, to see a big clod of dirt on Mother's grosgrain carpet. Johnny was looking in at them, color in his cheeks, his long, arching dark eyes less dull than usual. For a moment he looked as handsome and able as any young man.

"*Sue!*" Clare hissed. "*Do* something!"

"Um, Johnny." Sue's voice sounded weak and timid; she forced more strength into it. "Johnny, maybe you'd like to step around to the kitchen? Mother will give you . . . a glass of lemonade."

"I want to see Minnie," Johnny said, as if they might be hiding her.

"I'm sorry—"

"Go up to the Campbells' and see her," Clare said, with sudden energy. "Go to the *back* door."

Johnny's big shaggy head turned toward Clare. The room was quiet.

An emphatic bang from the kitchen as the oven door slipped from Mother's hand and sprang shut. Sue heard the slow hoofbeats of the big team out on the road.

Now Mother's quick steps came nearer. Sue opened her mouth to call a warning. Too late. Mother came into the hall, jumped, gasped, and pressed one hand to her heart. "*Johnny!* My goodness, you frightened me!"

Johnny's head turned slowly. He said nothing.

"I—how—is your mother well?" Mother caught sight of the boots on the carpet. Her mouth opened and closed, as she considered mentioning it.

"I came to see Minnie," Johnny said again. "I found out she was here."

The air in the room seemed to thicken like a jelly and hold them all suspended. He wanted what they did not have to give. He would stand there asking until the crack of doom.

In the extraordinary silence Sue heard a thump out in the yard, footsteps, and there was Ed behind Johnny, his face all alive, smiling that dangerous smile you see just before a fight. He tapped Johnny on the shoulder.

Johnny turned, fists bulging. The rug twisted and smeared.

"What can we do for you, Coombs?" Ed asked. Henry was coming quickly over the lawn, and Father was behind him.

"He came to see Minnie," Mother said before Johnny could answer. "But of course she's gone."

"Then I guess you'd better go, too!" Ed said. "At least step off my mother's rug." His voice sounded gentle, but the hall was full of big shoulders, crowding.

Nothing happened for a moment. Johnny's face was dark red; they could hear his breathing. Henry was pale and furious. Ed still smiled, a bright spot of color on each cheekbone.

Then Johnny said, in an unexpectedly soft voice, "Sorry. I didn't realize." He moved toward the front step, and Ed and Henry backed up to let him pass.

Mother jerked into motion and stepped to the door. "Johnny, wait! I'll send something along for your mother."

"Got to go, if I'm going to see Minnie," Johnny said, vanishing from Sue's range of vision.

"Lucky Minnie!" Henry muttered loudly. There was a sudden quiet. Was he coming back? Then hoofbeats, and the ugly white plowhorse in his dirty harness passed the door, Johnny on his back.

Mother let her breath out in a whoosh. "Boys, you might have handled that more tactfully! He didn't mean any harm."

"He was scaring the girls," Ed said.

"He wasn't scaring *me!*" Sue said indignantly, and would have said more, but for remembering that she'd almost fainted like a heroine in a novel.

Father said, "Nobody's got any need to be scared of Johnny Coombs—or to pick on him, either."

Ed's face reddened. "Well he's got to be kept in line, hasn't he? Letting him do whatever he wants—that's not treating him right, is it? That's not treating him like everybody else."

"Johnny doesn't do much of what he *wants,*" Father said. "For Tolman's sake, if nothing more, I'll have him treated kindly. All right?"

For Father, that was a harsh speech, and Ed looked down at his boots. Henry said, "I don't think you'd care for the way Johnny talks about girls, Captain, if you happened to hear it. But you won't. He only does it around young men. I tell you, he's not as much of a fool as you all think!"

"He's got *some* sense, anyway," Sue said. "He's picked Minnie to fall in love with."

Tsk! went Clare's tongue; just a tiny sound, quieter than a match strike. Sue stared for a second. The blood thundered in her ears.

"Don't you tsk! Minnie's worth *ten* of you! You don't mean to lift another finger—"

"*Susan!*" Mother said.

They all were looking at her. Their mouths hung open. Clare stood rigid, slender in her pale, fashionable dress, one hand pressed to the base of her throat. Sue's face grew hot, and hotter.

"Don't I smell something burning?" Clare asked at last, in a gently reminding voice.

"Oh! My biscuits!" Mother rushed away, and slowly everyone else followed, leaving Sue alone.

17

SUE FELT HER HANDS TREMBLE. A column of heat ran up the middle of her chest. It roared like a fire, and it felt *good*. The big hard lump that had weighed on her heart for two days was simply incinerated. She could breathe freely.

Out in the kitchen questions were being answered. The snatches Sue heard were of dresses, hotel dinners and hotel trappings, tennis matches watched from the lawn.

"Didn't you play?" Ed asked.

"Oh, no!" Clare said. "Neither of the Marys is very strong, and Julia and I found that the mountain air made us giddy."

You had your own game! Sue thought. On the farm, or where other young women were athletic, delicate health let Clare excuse herself and play the game she preferred, one of the graceful girls in white.

Pots clinked; spoons rattled. In the sharpness of the sounds Sue could hear Mother's anger. But Clare's voice went on, light, smooth, with a new cultivated sound, new prinks and curlicues. She's smoothing Mother, Sue realized. What does she want?

"So, Mother,"—Here it came!—"Aunt Emma's probably going to ask me to visit them in Boston this winter. Isn't that nice of her?"

She was supposed to ask *me*, Sue thought. But she didn't feel astonished. There was nothing surprising about this.

"Has she invited you?" Mother asked, with some constraint in her voice.

"No, but she mentioned it. She wouldn't have done that if she weren't nearly certain."

"I wouldn't set my heart on it, Clare," Mother said. "People like the Campbells have the wherewithal to change their plans rapidly."

"But if Sue is well enough—"

"Just a minute, Clare," Mother interrupted. A moment later she came in and put Sue's tray down on the table with a bang. "Susan, I'd like to know what on *earth* has gotten into you!"

Sue stared back at her, meeting the hard brilliance of Mother's eyes with a hardness of her own. You don't have any idea, do you? she thought. You simply can't imagine!

But after a moment tears began to prickle in her hard, dry eyes. She wasn't up to the strain of defying Mother. She felt her face flush, and she whispered, without quite meaning to, "I miss Minnie."

Mother sighed, the way she sighed when Ed plugged the watermelons or Henry wouldn't stop talking or any of them quarreled. "Minnie will be back here every Monday. In the meantime you could make an effort to get along with your sister!"

"Why? Why is Minnie coming Mondays?"

"I need help with the washing," Mother said, "and your aunt can spare her."

"But can't Clare—"

Mother glanced away, as if embarrassment just brushed her with its sleeve in passing. "I don't want to risk Clare's health. She's looking pale—"

"She's pale because she hardly set foot outdoors in three weeks!"

"Clare's health has always been delicate—"

"*Mother!* Half the time she's faking so *I'll* do the work!"

"Susan Gorham!" Mother said. "I don't want to hear another word of this! It would hardly do your sister much good to fake sickness *now*, would it?"

Now! The word rang on in the suddenly quiet room with a bitter sound. *Now* outside help must be brought in. *Now* the special, long-cherished formulation of the family was spoiled.

But that's not true! Sue thought. Faking sickness would do Clare nearly as much good as it always had. It would cost Mother more. That was the only difference.

After Clare had gone to bed, Sue lay staring at the white door between them. Her eyes burned. She heard Clare undress, heard each little sound she made settling into bed.

You are *not* going to Boston, she thought through the door, like a bullet. You are *not* going. I won't let you. The column up her center was like a smelting furnace, and she was glad of it. It annealed her heart against all hurt and prevented her from crying.

Her legs ached. They wanted to get moving. They could carry her now, but no one knew. Right here, she thought. I'm staying right here until something in this family changes.

18

FOR THE NEXT FOUR DAYS Sue lay implacably on the couch. She didn't sit up for meals, only propped herself on her elbow. She didn't knit, although her jersey was nearly finished and she had been eager to wear it. She just lay on the pillow, watched, and listened.

The house was full of struggle. Mother needed Clare's help, and everything Clare did inhibited her from asking. It ranged from putting on a slightly nicer than everyday dress the morning after her return, to the writing of letters to new friends each evening on the best paper, to the way she held her head, the way she walked. Mother responded by doing the hardest jobs herself, asking Clare to help only with the easy work. Clare was winning that struggle.

But she won't beat *me*, Sue thought. They had been struggling for three years now, since Clare's return from that first trip with Aunt Emma, and Sue had never, ever won. She hadn't been allowed to. She was the older sister and must protect the younger. She was well, and Clare was sick.

This time she would not lose. She felt hard inside, and her eyes were hard as pebbles when they looked at Clare. Her body surged with energy. It was all she could do not to get up and pace the floor.

She didn't think of Boston. It would be nice to see something of the wider world, but it was here that mattered. Here in Westminster West the change had to be made.

"I can't *stand* it!" Minnie whispered Monday morning. "The way she presses her hand—" Minnie's own wet red hand left a damp spot on her calico dress, just below the neckline. "You should have seen her at church! Herb Phillips has this big burn across the back of his hand, and she saw it, and—'oh, my!' " Minnie pressed her hand to her throat again.

"I know," Sue said. She had witnessed every one of Clare's mannerisms: the new way of holding a book, the new way of sitting in a chair, as if to accommodate a bigger bustle than Clare actually possessed. Did these gestures play well in a resort hotel? In Westminster West they seemed absurd, but evidently not to Mother.

Mother is a fool! Sue thought. But that was unbearable. "What's the news?" she asked.

"Oh, the big news! Julia's finally gotten your aunt to take her to Europe!"

"*Europe!*" The word expanded and shivered on the air, like the sound of the clock striking. Europe . . .

"They decided last night," Minnie said. "Your aunt doesn't want to because it'll be almost a year, but Julia won. They're taking a steamer sometime in November."

Then Boston was out of the question. "Does Clare know?"

"I suppose she knows by now!" Minnie said. Clare had gone to the Campbell house to spend the day.

"Minnie?" Mother called from the yard. "I'm ready to wring these out."

Europe! Sue thought, listening to Minnie laugh with

Mother and the splash of water in the old zinc catch basin. They wouldn't ask Clare to go, would they? A vacation in the White Mountains, a few weeks in Boston—that was one thing. A year in Europe was quite another.

"So, I've put a stop to Johnny Coombs," Minnie said over dinner. Sue looked up in confusion.

"Put a *stop*?"

"Yes! I told him I was engaged."

"To who?" Sue gasped.

"Nobody, silly! I didn't say who. I said it was a secret, but I had to be fair to him, I had to tell him, and he wasn't to tell a soul. Poor thing—I did feel sorry for him."

"Minnie . . . will *you* go to Europe?"

Minnie looked startled. "No. Why would they take a hired girl? They'll do for each other on the boat and hire a maid over there, I suppose. It's a great cost, you know, even for people like the Campbells."

Then of course they wouldn't take Clare.

"You do look strange this morning, Sue. Are you all right? How's your walking?"

They might take *Clare* as a maid. They wouldn't have to pay her, the way they would Minnie.

"*Are* you walking?"

How loud and insistent Minnie sounded! Sue shook her head.

"*What? Why not?*"

Sue grasped at random for an explanation. "Clare's a light sleeper. I'm afraid I'll wake her."

"You're joking!" Minnie gasped. "*Susie!*"

But if neither she nor Clare could go to Boston, then they

both would stay here. And if they stayed, things *must* be fairer. It was more important than ever. "*What*, Minnie? What do you keep going on about?"

Minnie sat back with an offended look. "I was saying I think you're crazy! But never mind!"

Sue stretched out her hand. "No, Minnie. Don't get mad. I'm just—"

"Crazy," Minnie said when Sue couldn't go on. She took Sue's hand, though, and gave it a short, sharp squeeze.

Clare had *not* been asked to go to Europe. Sue knew as soon as Clare came through the parlor late that afternoon, walking stiffly and slowly as if her bones might break. The change of plans must have been a great shock, and of course she couldn't show that. All day Clare must have been obliged to conceal her feelings. She walked straight into her room and closed the door.

A moment later Mother came into the parlor. "Clare? Would you mind making biscuits so I can take care of the milk?" As always at the end of washday Mother was bone tired.

Silence. Then Clare said, "Yes. I'll do them." She opened the door. Her eyes looked bruised.

"No, Clare, you rest," Mother decided, and for once Sue couldn't blame her. Clare looked really ill.

But she said quickly, "No, no. I can do them!"

I'll do them, Sue thought. She found herself sitting upright, braced to stand. Mother looked astonished.

"Susan? Do you need something? Don't move—I'll get it."

"I—" The floor spun slightly, sank a little. It would steady, if she waited.

She glanced up and saw Clare watching her with wide eyes, pupils growing larger and larger. Looking past Sue. Looking at the sofa.

Oh, no, you don't! Sue thought instantly. Mother was watching her, too, so worn and old-looking. Suddenly Sue couldn't bear their eyes upon her, couldn't bear to look into their faces.

She said, "I need to go back upstairs."

19

AFTER SUPPER, after she had washed the dishes, set the table, and swept the kitchen floor, Mother climbed slowly up the stairs and made Sue's bed. Her feet scuffed wearily on the steps, and Sue shrank at the sound. This was more work for Mother; everything was more work for Mother.

But in ten minutes the bed was ready, and Mother called, "David, will you bring Sue up?"

Ed looked up in surprise. "Leaving us?" He glanced at Clare's rocker. But Clare had gone early to bed.

"Yes," Sue said. "I . . . it's not that comfortable."

"I had an idea you were getting better," Henry said with a frown.

"Sue can get better upstairs just as well as she can down here," Father said, carefully marking his place in *The Agriculturist*.

He approached the couch, slid one arm behind Sue's back and the other beneath her knees, and lifted her. "Hang on."

Belatedly it occurred to Sue that one of the boys should take her, that Father was not young. Henry said suddenly, "I'll do that, Captain!"

But no one could deny Father's physical strength. So much had been asked of him when young, and he'd always given it. His muscles were like iron, his step steady on the stairs:

left, right, left, right. . . . Even at the point of putting Sue down, the point at which a burden is heaviest, his arms didn't tremble and his movement was smooth. Sue left her arms around his neck a moment longer than necessary, so he would know it was a hug. "Thank you," she whispered.

"I'll come up with my knitting in a minute," Mother said.

"No," Sue said quickly. "I—I don't mind being alone."

Mother closed her eyes. Any other day of the week she would have insisted. But sometimes Mondays were too much, even for Mother. "I'll send up the rest of your things. Good night."

It was Ed who brought them. "This is all pretty hard on Mother," he said abruptly.

"Yes," Sue said.

Ed looked at her sharply and then sighed, shoving his hands in his pockets, roaming around the room. "I don't understand this. Why does everything in this family seem so . . ." He paused by the window, struggling for a word. "I don't know, like everybody's *stuck!* Is it always like this in the fall? I'm usually at academy by now. Does this always happen?"

Go away, Sue thought. Ed's ignorance made him seem childish tonight. "No. This doesn't happen."

"Then what's going on? Why aren't you better? Why the heck doesn't somebody send you to a specialist? How long have you been in bed, Susie?"

Sue closed her eyes. "Ed. Please." They don't send for a specialist because Mother *expects* to have a sick child. Because she knows, maybe, that it's not real anymore. Because . . . just because.

"*God!*" Ed said suddenly, almost violently. "Sometimes all I want is *out* of here! I can't wait till January!" Sue heard his steps go down the stairs. The room grew still. She opened her eyes on its familiar bareness.

What are you doing? she asked herself, and no answer came. She only knew that she was not strong enough to stay on the sofa and face Clare's tragic look, Mother's exhaustion. And she would not get up yet. She couldn't.

Ed and Henry came upstairs to bed. All sounds died away. Sue sat up straight, put her feet down on the cool floorboards, and stood. She touched the bedpost. It was there to support her if she needed it, but she did not. She felt the sturdy, reliable locking of her knees, the strength of her thigh muscles, the good stretch in her spine. Her stomach muscles trembled slightly. They were weak, but they would hold.

Carefully, touching the one bedpost as long as possible and reaching for the other, she walked all the way around the end of the bed and got in on the other side. There!

In the morning she knew why she was up here: Clare bringing up the tray with swollen, downcast eyes, still with that look of shock. Your life is *here*, Clare, she thought. When you start doing your share, I'll get up to help you. She was doing something wrong. She knew that. But someone had to make it happen. Downstairs she wouldn't be able to wait. She'd feel too sorry for Clare.

Preserving was in full swing, and the house smelled of pickles, apples, spice. For days Mother was too busy to carry work up to the bedroom. Sue often heard her calling for Clare, but she couldn't tell how much Clare helped or how willingly. When Clare brought meals, she was very quiet, as if her shock were still fresh. But time was passing. Get over it, Sue thought at her. Get over it, and I'll be there to help. She waited for signs of that, waited, and walked.

Softly, her bare feet making no sound or jar, she wandered the room, observing the rumpled runner on the table, the light film of dust that had begun to gather on the woodwork since Minnie's departure—only looking, since to straighten or dust anything would be to give herself away. Her clothes in the closet had been so long unworn they seemed to belong to someone else. The dresses hung limply on their pegs. Dust had gathered on the folds of her riding skirt. In the back of the closet were her boots; jammed down inside one was the red book. She left it there.

Often she stood near the window, watching the busy, orderly farmyard, sun glimmering on the ice pond, sheep, cattle and horses grazing, the oat harvest coming in. Behind the shoulder of the barn the hill yellowed, and the trees turned dull green and then suddenly, overnight, flared to scarlet and gold.

Once she whistled to Bright as he drank from the barnyard trough. He raised his head sharply, looking toward the house, and Ed, who'd just turned him loose, looked, too. Sue stepped quickly back from the window.

Bright. Bright remembered her.

Nights she dreamed, but she didn't know of what. When she awakened, she could sometimes hear her own gasp on the dark air. The bed would spin and spin, like a leaf adrift on a stream. It swooped, it swirled, and she clutched the sheet beneath her until her hands hurt, listening to the pounding of her own heart, the melodic interruptions of the big clock downstairs. She kept no account of time. It seemed better not to.

But one morning a cold freshness, a smell of fallen leaves

came in on the air. Sue walked silently to the head of the stairs and looked down. It was baking day. She could hear the brisk squeak of the rolling pin under Mother's hands, catch the dusty scent of flour. Her hands longed to make a piecrust or shape a loaf of bread.

She touched one hand to the banister, grasped the smooth, cool wood firmly. Her toes actually hung over the top stair. She was ready to take the first step—

"Clare? This isn't quite enough apple, and I'm up to my elbows in piecrust. Can you quick chop some more?"

A sigh from the front parlor. Sue drew back. A moment later Clare came through the hall. Her shoulders sagged, and her hair, to Sue's surprise, was carelessly arranged and rather untidy. She couldn't see Clare's face, but suddenly Clare looked up the stairs. Her mouth was contorted in a wide grimace, like a little child crying. "Damn you, Sue!" she whispered. "Come *down!*"

Sue's heart pounded. She stood very still. Clare went on to the kitchen. Slowly Sue realized that Clare had not seen her.

I will go down, she thought, getting back into bed. And she would! When, was the only question. She must do it right, at the right time. She wasn't giving up. She wasn't losing the fight. She was—

You *can't* go down!

The thought was like a separate voice in her head, new and startling. Nonsense! she thought immediately. Of course she could, whenever she wanted to. This afternoon or tomorrow.

No, you can't. You want to stay up here. You can't make yourself want to go down.

"I can, too!" Sue whispered. "I can go right now!"

106

Is that so?

"Yes!" Sue said aloud, and stood up. The quickness of the motion made her giddy, and in the cool air her legs crawled with gooseflesh. What would she put on? Get back in bed while she decided.

See?

No. I can do whatever I want!

But what do you want? You *want* to stay right here.

Sue curled in bed and put her fingers in her ears. But the voice was within and kept on speaking in a dull, neutral tone, in time with her pulse. Cra-zy cra-zy cra-zy cra—

"Susie? I'm sorry, was you asleep?"

Aunt Mary Braley stood at the bedside, all apuff from the long climb up the stairs. Sue sat up, shaking her head. "No. No, I—"

"Heard you was abed again, and I was on my way by. Been seein' Em'ly and Laura off. I've prevailed on Em'ly to accept money from me and take poor Laura to the seashore. They say it does good sometimes."

"How is Laura?" Sue asked, grasping at good manners for help.

Aunt Mary shook her head very slightly. "It's hard for me to keep my hopes up. I've seen this too often. But how are you, Susie? Do you feel as if you're gettin' better?"

Sue drew a breath that went on and on as she realized she did not have an answer. "I—don't know." Was it better to be dizzy or to have voices?

Aunt Mary's old eyes were the color of brook water in the spring, a surprising green, and they flashed for a moment with a look of speculation. But all she said was, "You'll get well in your own good time. Don't fret about the work; your mother says it's well in hand."

Sue couldn't answer. Aunt Mary glanced at her and then settled herself in the bedside chair. "I was up by Coombses' yesterday," she said after a moment. "Trouble on my mind, I guess. All I could think of was poor Homer Miller."

It took a moment for the name to penetrate. Not Johnny Coombs. Homer Miller. "Did you know him?"

Aunt Mary looked down at her lap. After a moment she said quietly, "Ever'body was very sorry for his father when it happened. I remember in church people took his hand, but us children took a different view of it. In those days children didn't disobey their parents, but I remember thinking, *I* won't stand in front of an oxcart for *anybody!* And I never have."

"What do you mean?" Sue asked almost in a whisper.

"He should have stepped out of the way," Aunt Mary said soberly. "Let the old oxen run! I've done that, you know. Went to nurse durin' the war, and when I felt I had to, I come home. And after Mr. Braley died, and I was told I should sell out—and I felt as though that would kill me—well, I stayed put. Some people didn't think that was right. My own children! But you don't have to let yourself be run over, Susie. Over the years I've come to feel very free."

Sue felt the words go through her with a piercing ache and sweetness. I've come to feel very free.

Then Aunt Mary said, "But you know, Bela would have torn a strip off of poor Homer if he'd let those oxen run. A parent don't always think what they're askin' or how a child understands."

"I know," Sue said.

Aunt Mary slowly nodded. "Yes," she said. "Well, Homer'd be an old man now, and Bela's with us yet. It's like Reverend Stevens said, nothing stands still. That's the one thing you can count on."

When Aunt Mary was gone, Sue paced the floor silently. I'll get up if I can be like Mary Braley, she thought. What do you think I am? she could ask Mother, the next time she asked too much, the next time she forgot to be fair. What do you think I am? That should bring Mother up short!

Tomorrow was Thursday, cleaning day. She would go downstairs tomorrow. She could slip into the work of the day without anyone noticing.

But Thursday came, and Sue still waited. Waited? Or was caught, like a fly on flypaper? How could she tell if she was caught except by trying?

How could she try when she just didn't want to?

She didn't go down, and Thursday night came.

20

WITH A GASP Sue awakened to lie on the spinning bed, watching the yellow light flicker on the windowpane. . . .

Yellow light flickering on the windowpane.

Yellow light?

Sue sat up. She was still dreaming.

Was she? The air was chilly on her shoulders, and her hair hung down her back, in her eyes. But in the top corner of the window a light continued to dance. It looked very real, like little flames reflected—

Her feet hit the floor with a slap; she stood up; her knees weakened and buckled, but she fell on them next to the window. The flames were out there, at the back corner of the big barn, the sheep barn, the chicken house, big as bonfires, and growing.

"*Fire!*" Her voice came out in a loud, powerful shout as she rose. She ran out to the hall. "Father! Henry! The barns are on fire! *Father!*"

Throughout the house came startled thumps and crashes. As Sue turned back to her room, Henry raced past in his nightshirt, trying to shove his feet into his boots in midrun. Ed followed, barefoot and pulling on his trousers. The front door banged open.

Sue was at her closet door, stripping off her nightgown.

Her riding skirt was nearest; she pulled it on, fighting hooks and eyes. Jersey. She pushed her feet into her boots. One wouldn't go in—the red book. She shook it out, and it fell with a small thump in the back corner of the closet.

The big door stood wide open at the bottom of the stairs. The banister glided beneath her hand; her boots rapped like snare drums. She passed Clare in the doorway of the parlor, a white blur in her nightgown.

Outside, the night was blazing orange and loud with the lick of flames. Father, Ed, and Henry drove the sheep from the barn. The merinos baaed and huddled, heads high, ears back, and let themselves be driven as one animal toward the big field.

"The horses!" Sue screamed. "Are the horses out?"

Father turned, a black silhouette against the flickering light. "In the night pasture!" he shouted.

Then the cows were out, too. What else? A shriek of hens, a wild flutter. Mother behind the flaming chicken house window in her dressing gown, shooing hens from their perches.

The hogs! Sue ran to their pen, on the ground floor of the big barn. The hogs were screaming, but the fire was in the far corner. It had not reached them.

She struggled with the latch. The hogs crowded against the gate, putting so much pressure on the hasp that she couldn't draw it back. *"Move!"* she screamed. *"Move!"*

Her screams were nothing to theirs. She couldn't even hear herself. She snatched up a piece of sacking draped on a post and flapped it over the hogs' backs. The tide of flesh receded for a moment, and she tore the latch open, fingernails breaking. "Go *on!*"

The hogs needed no driving. They surged out the gate, all trying to crowd through at once, and raced into the blackness.

For a moment the barn seemed quiet, with only the laughing, happy sound of the flames. They roared up the huge posts and across the underside of the floorboards, yellow and orange and lovely. Could they really be killing the barn?

Sue ran out after the hogs. Now what? She couldn't think what to do next.

Father raced past her, straight into the big barn. A moment later he brought a harness to the doorway. Mother was suddenly there and dragged it away. Henry and Ed had rolled the heavy wagon out and were pushing it off into the dark. Now Father gave the buggy a shove, and it rolled out on its own, shafts skating across the dirt. A barn cat leaped off the seat and disappeared into the night.

Sue caught at the spokes as the buggy slowed. She tried to push it up the road. It would only turn in a circle, but then Ed was there at the other wheel.

"Henry!" Father shouted. "Pump some water and watch the corners of the house!"

Sue whirled to look as Henry sprinted past. The heat buffeted her face; it hadn't been anywhere near that bad when she'd first run out the door. The house was still all right, but flames ballooned out around the sheep barn, so close.

"Tell Clare to pump!" she yelled at Henry, and turned back to Ed. "Can't we get water from the ice pond?"

Ed just shook his head, coughing, as they ran back toward the barns. No, of course not. They couldn't get the water up, with only five of them to span the whole distance. No time to harness a horse, even if they could catch one. The pond, not five hundred yards from the burning barn, was useless.

Something sailed out of the barn doorway in a glittering arc and landed on the pile of harness.

Bright's nickel-studded bridle.

21

SUE HAD THE bridle in her hand and was running toward the barway before she knew what she meant to do. It was cooler, blacker, quieter, over here. She banged hard against the poles and whistled for Bright. Out across the dark pasture she heard drumming hooves, grunts, the low, drawn-out, wavering bawl of a cow in full gallop.

She whistled again, slid back the top bar, slid back the bottom. Would Bright come? *Toward* the fires, toward the uproar, when she hadn't called him in so long?

She whistled a third time, leaning on the middle bar to rest her shaking legs. If he didn't come, could she *run* all the way to the Holdens'?

Hoofbeats in the darkness. Bright stopped ten feet away, with a loud, frightened, challenging snort.

"Bright! It's me."

He hesitated. Firelight gleamed on the round curves of his back, and his nostrils were huge black caverns. His little ears flicked back and forward.

Then he took a step toward her. Sue slipped under the rail and put the reins around his neck. He took the bit, staring past her at the flames arching high over the sheep barn roof. The stench of burning wool nearly made Sue vomit. Thank God the sheep were out. Only the fleeces were burning.

"*No*, David! You can't let her!"

Father had seen her run, had understood. He was at the gate now, taking down the last bar. Mother, behind him, reached for his arm. He paid no attention.

"Bring him through, Susie!" Bright's front feet seemed nailed to the ground. Father's voice rang out. "Bright! *Hup!*"

Bright trembled, then danced forward, crowding against Sue, almost dragging her along. He hopped the bars and stopped again, eyes bulging as he stared at the flaming barns. Sue remembered: A horse will run back to a burning stable. But Bright lived mostly in the pasture; he shuddered and danced away from the sight of the barn in flames.

"You'll be all right?" Father's hand was on the bridle, his other hand making a stirrup. Sue put her foot into his hand, and he threw her up. Bright's back sank and surged, but Father held him firm. Sue reached up to wind the reins around her hands and bury her fingers deep in Bright's long mane.

"Holden's, then Campbell's—tell them to bring force pumps. Then Drislane and Hall. *Hang on!*"

He let the bridle go, and Bright leaped away in a spray of gravel. His muscles bunched, his hoofbeats were one long drum roll, and Sue had no grip on his back. She was carried along on his airstream, her legs slipping farther and farther back. She pulled herself forward, closed her legs around him. Straight as an arrow up the deeply shadowed road gallopingallopingalloping . . .

Like an explosion, he shied to the right. Sue felt herself flying loose. Only one leg was still around him, stretching like a piece of elastic, out into thin air. She was coming off . . .

No. Her fingers hurt, but they were deep in his mane, and she pulled herself straight on his round, slippery back as he

114

galloped up the little rise. The hill slowed him but not enough. At the turn she would fall.

"Bright!" she gasped. "Whoa!" To shorten the reins, she had to free her hands from his tangling mane. One, quickly the other. She wrapped the reins once more around her fists and pressed them hard to the muscle of his neck. "Bright, *whoa!*"

He didn't whoa, but the hard-driving gallop hesitated. A float and a lift came into it. She could sit to it now and free her hands, check and release, check and release, and by the time he reached the main road he was trotting. Sue turned him downhill.

Now canter again. In the moonlight Sue could see the Holdens' barn, almost a quarter mile away. Bright's hooves sounded like gunfire on the road. She could hear his great, gasping breaths. In the sky an orange light seemed to reach from behind, like a huge cupped hand trying to catch them.

They rounded the corner, passed the barn, and clattered up to the dark house. For just a second it felt strange and wrong to disturb the quiet. Would she be able to yell? Bright stopped in two hard bounces, snorting loudly and Sue fought for breath.

An upstairs window crashed up. Jerome Holden leaned out, the sash pushing his nightcap askew. "Fire!" Sue gasped. "The barns!"

"Firebug?"

"Yes," Sue said. Three fires at once—it could only be the firebug. Bright whirled beneath her, and she slipped and clutched his mane. The sky above the hill glowed; sparks rose. What was happening? "Force pumps!" she shouted to the empty window, and Mrs. Holden's head popped out.

115

"Susie Gorham, as I live and breathe! Hang *on* to that black devil!"

Sue found herself laughing as she cantered down the driveway. Devil? There was never a better horse than Bright. He'd come to her out of the night pasture; he carried her safely. . . . Her heart swelled. "Oh, Bright!"

He swooped around the corner onto the Westminster West road. Now they were coming to the burned-out Campbell barn. That would scare him in the moonlight. Sue laced her fingers deep in his mane. But Bright cantered past without swerving, and Sue turned him up the driveway of the pillared mansion.

"Wake up! Fire!" She didn't have enough breath, Bright wouldn't stand. "At Gorham's—fire. *Aunt Emma! Uncle Fred!*"

A back window flew up. "*Susie!*" It was Minnie.

"The *barns* are on fire!" Sue screamed. "Force pumps!" Lights were coming on all through the long house. Bright whirled on the gravel.

Sue let him gallop around the corner, past the Holden house, all awake now. Ahead on the road, horses were running, Mr. Holden and someone else racing to the fire. Bright caught them as they started to climb the hill, then thundered past. Past their own road, glowing like a fireplace; he would have turned there, but Sue kept him running. His breath whistled, his mane stung her eyes, and Sue could feel him slow and strain as the steep, heartbreakingly long hill drained the strength from him.

They crested the hill between the two giant hayfields. Here the moon shone white and serene, and the road was flat. Bright's gallop was slower and not as steady, as Sue turned him up the drive to the Drislanes'.

116

Moonlight shone full on the sheltered front porch and on the timbers of the new barn. Sue rode up close to the house. "Fire! Fire at Gorham's!" Loud enough? No one was coming. . . .

"Saints above, it's Susie Gorham!"

At once Sue turned Bright down the driveway. One look at the sky would answer all questions.

Bright's sides heaved, and his back was no longer slippery. Sue's legs and skirt were welded to him with sweat. She turned down the road toward the Hall house, white and silent in the moonlight. She needed to brace her hands against his neck now. Her legs seemed to have no strength left.

Up the driveway—no yell left either. She drew Bright close to the front door and reached for the rope that rang the dinner bell. It clanged. Bright shuddered away, and Sue let him go down the driveway. Behind her voices. "Who's th— Oh." A shout, and feet thumping through the house. "Fire down at Gorham's! Wake up!"

The glow in the sky was enormous. Sue rode slowly toward it. The house must be afire, too. Was Clare out? Surely they all were safe?

But she couldn't hurry now. Bright jigged for a moment, then dropped to a fast, jerky walk. He trotted again, briefly, when the Halls galloped past, but slowed without any signal from Sue. His part was done, and tenderly, taking care of himself and Sue, Bright minced down the hill and turned in at the farm road.

A great flickering light filled the road before them. Bright hesitated and then went on. Sue clung, leaning forward on his hot, sticky neck. Down the little hill and around the corner toward the roaring flames.

The heat struck her in the face. Bright stopped in his tracks, and it was like standing in front of the range on baking day. The heat came in waves, making a wind of its own. The house was still standing, but the roof glowed red—no, that was just reflection. Someone was pumping water on the slates, someone was up there watching, but the house was untouched.

Where the sheep barn had stood, a great bonfire roared. The big barn was just a shell, red and flaming inside and out. The huge timbers stood out dark, like a skeleton.

As Sue sat watching, the roof collapsed. There was a crash, shouts. Father was moving people back, directing people with pumps and buckets and a gathering tank on a wagon. The people looked tiny against the huge fires, like toy soldiers, and Father was like a toy captain, but all alive, with a crisp look of command and a spring to his step.

Once they all had moved to where he wanted them, Father turned, looking up the road. For a moment he stood there with his back to the inferno. Just as Sue understood and moved Bright forward into the light, he saw her.

His whole frame relaxed, and he came running. Passing one of the young Holden boys, who had been made to stand back out of the way, he clapped him on the arm and brought him along. "Whoa, Bright. Young fellow, hang on to this horse's bridle."

Father's face was red with reflected firelight, and tears glittered on his cheeks, catching the flames' brightness. He reached up for her. "Come on, Susie."

Sue tried to slide off. Her skirt stuck to Bright's back, and she had to free it with her hands before she could let herself down into Father's arms.

He pulled her close, deep, into the strongest hug she'd ever

118

felt, holding her whole weight for a moment and pressing his cheek against her hair. "Good girl. Good girl." Then he let her down.

Her feet touched the ground, and her knees buckled. She held on to his arm and made them straighten.

"Son," Father said to the Holden boy, "I want you to walk this horse cool. Keep him close to the fire, so he doesn't take a chill." He looked into the boy's face. "Now, this is your job. I'm counting on you to keep this horse from getting sick."

The boy's eyes were wide. He nodded solemnly and turned away, leading Bright in a small circle within the fire's glow.

"Your mother's in the house, Susie. With the sheep barn down, we think it's safe."

Sue heard his voice as if from a distance. How strange, the sheep barn being down was a good thing. They went together up the walk, where the firelight shone on the lavender and southernwood. The shouts and the loud flames seemed far away.

"Go on in. Can you make it by yourself?"

Sue glanced up at him. He was looking toward his barns, so interested, so aware that his face seemed almost glad. He dropped Sue's arm and turned away, and Sue walked in through the open kitchen door.

"*Sue!* Thank goodness!" Mother seized her by the shoulders with fingers that bit deep and looked searchingly into her face. Mother's eyes were wild and bloodshot, and her face was streaked diagonally with soot.

Sue burst out laughing.

"Young lady, don't you *dare* get hysterical!" Mother almost pushed her into the rocker. She snatched the shawl off the back of the chair and tucked it around Sue's shoulders, then turned to the sink to pump a cup full of water.

Laughter, or something, still shook Sue's body. Her mind felt calm. She felt like herself. But shudder after shudder ran through her, and when she took the cup, she shook so hard that a big slop of water landed on her lap.

Mother's hand closed around the cup, but Mother's hand shook, too. They stared at their hands, apparently wrestling for the cup.

Then Mother began to laugh. She laughed until her tears washed two clean paths down her cheeks. She brushed the tears away, making such a grotesque pattern that Sue laughed even harder and spilled the rest of the water on the floor.

"Oh, my goodness!" Mother gasped as their laughter died. "Oh! At least no one came in and saw us!" She got off her knees, stiffly, and went back to the pump for more water.

Sue looked around the kitchen. Sooty puddles stood on the scrubbed boards. A chair was tipped over. In the middle of the room were two bushel baskets half full of china and towels, ready to go if the house caught fire. Yet the table was still set for breakfast, with plates and cups turned upside down and all the silverware in order, exactly the way Sue had set it herself the evening before she got sick.

A great crash came from outside. Mother stepped to the door and stood looking for a few minutes. Then she came back, bringing the cup half full of water. "The south wall's down. That's a mercy."

"Was the boy still walking Bright?"

"Having trouble, but he still had hold of him."

Sue took a sip of water. "We should close the door," she said. "Keep the smoke out."

When the door was shut, it was suddenly quiet inside the kitchen. Despite the mess and the smell of smoke, it seemed like a sanctuary again, the women's room. Mother turned from the door, and Sue asked, quietly, the question she'd been afraid to ask till now: "Where is Clare?"

Mother met Sue's eyes. A flush came up under the streaks of soot, and her mouth set in a long, downcurved, trembling line. Sue's heart sank for a moment. Then Mother said, "Clare . . . is in bed."

22

CLICK! WENT the kitchen clock, as sharply and suddenly as a trap springing shut. But it was only time passing, second by second as always.

"Has she—was she—" Sue stopped, closed her eyes, and took a long breath, swallowing the questions.

Mother's voice was so low Sue could hardly hear. "When we didn't see her, we went looking. Your father went into the barn." Mother shuddered and pressed her hands to her face. "But Ed—Ed said, 'Look in the house,' and he found her."

"Is she—" No, there were no questions she could ask. Clare was not hurt. She had not overworked. What she had done was claim her place again. That moment in the hallway was suddenly more vivid to Sue than it had been while it was happening. Herself thundering down the stairs and Clare looking at *her*, not out at the fire but up at her sister with a wide, mesmerized stare.

"I've done wrong by Clare," Mother said, staring straight ahead. "Let her think she was delicate, let her get ideas. I should have realized long ago. I've done very wrong by both of you."

She sat at the table, so suddenly it was like a collapse, and put her head on her arms, right on top of a place setting.

Sue pulled herself out of the chair. Her legs trembled, and her thighs felt disastrously weak, as if the bones were gone. She crossed the room and put an arm around Mother's shoulders. Mother's back was unyielding, like the shell of a turtle. Sue felt a piercing sadness. She had wanted Mother to see, but she hadn't wanted it to hurt like this.

She kissed the back of Mother's head, the smoky, tangled, slept-on hair. Then she went to Clare's room.

There was no lamp lit in the back bedroom, but the moonlight poured in across the bed, spread with Clare's lacy white afghan, across Clare in her nightgown. Her face had an exalted look, as if here, where not even the light of the fires penetrated, she participated in the excitement with all of them.

"Susie! Was it the firebug?"

The question left Sue staring blankly. She could smell herself, reeking of horse sweat and smoke in this clean, still room. She had meant to scream at Clare; it had felt like a scream inside her. *How can you do this to them? Do you know Father risked his life to find you?*

But suddenly that seemed impossible. What Clare had done was no different from what Sue had done.

Yes, it is different, some part of her asserted.

Not that different. Lie in bed through a season of work. Go to bed while the barns burned down. A difference, but where was the line? She could not scream at Clare because she herself was guilty. Mother of course had not screamed either, and it was worse for Mother. Sue had known for a month now that she was doing something wrong. Mother had never suspected it of herself until just this moment.

"Yes, Clare," she said. "It was the firebug. I'd better go see what's happening."

123

* * *

Father was just going out the kitchen door, carrying a kettle, and Mother was taking cups out of the cupboard. "Check in those baskets, Sue," she said, not turning. "How many people are out there?"

Sue dropped on her knees beside the baskets. "What is he doing?"

"He's making coffee! No sense heating up the cookstove, he said, when we've got all that fire outside. You'd think this happened every day. I'll never understand him!"

I feel that way about everyone, Sue thought, and at the same time she felt as if she understood them all perfectly.

The world had gone gray and grainy, and she couldn't tell if it was tiredness or smoke. Her hands kept taking things out of the basket, as if they had minds of their own.

Mother bent over her to take the cups. "Of all things!" she said. "I was going to save my dishcloth!"

They emptied out one basket and put in all the cups, the old tin ones, the agateware, and the thick white mugs they drank from every day. "I'll take them," Mother said, but Sue kept hold of one handle, and they carried the basket together. The boneless feeling had spread up Sue's back, down her legs. How strange that she could keep on moving anyway, that she could balance and heft the basket and open the door with her free hand.

The scene outside was strangely peaceful. The sheep barn seemed like the large, friendly bonfire at the Grange corn roast. The big barn made a bigger blaze, but it seemed to know its place and didn't threaten to spread. And the chicken house fire was the perfect size for cooking.

Men stood watchfully, pumps and buckets ready, but the

shouting was over. Just friendly, excited talk now. ". . . thought I was a goner when that timber went," Sue heard, and, "By golly, about the time my beard started to smoking I figured I'd get out!"

It must be just like the war, she thought, like the aftermath of battle.

Near the big barn stood the generals: Father, Fred Campbell, Patrick Drislane. Drislane did not usually belong because he was an Irishman, a Catholic, but his barn had been burned, too, making him at least the equal of Jerome Holden, who so far had lost nothing. A little space was allowed to exist between them and the rest. They stood in a close group, their shoulders and their hatbrims at an angle of authority.

The water in the kettle began to smell like coffee. A cloud of smoke drifted over, drifted back. In the east, above the low ridge, the sky was beginning to lighten.

The generals turned slowly, as one man, and wandered toward the coffee kettle. ". . . hire a detective," Father was saying.

"Now why do we need some Boston detective?" Jerome Holden asked passionately. "We know the ground, we know every gol—everybody in town! Why can't we handle it ourselves?"

"We haven't made much of a job of it so far," Campbell commented. At this early hour, shrugged into an old frock coat, he didn't look any richer or more important than anyone else.

They stopped by the kettle. "Well now, Susie, what a night of it you've had!" Patrick Drislane said.

Jerome Holden said, "You could have knocked me down with a feather when I realized 'twas Susie Gorham out there! Didn't know you was up and around."

125

Sue looked down at her feet. What was she supposed to say?

Father, with just a glance at her, said, "She got you folks here, didn't she?"

"David," Mother asked, looking skeptically into the kettle, "is this substance going to be drinkable?"

"I drank it for four years," Father said, "and when I couldn't get it, I chewed dry grounds."

Jerome Holden chuckled. "If there's one thing I hate, Gorham, it's a man who drags a war story into every conversation!"

The coffee was dreadfully bitter, even with cream. Father drank his black. He'd grown silent, staring into the flames with his hands wrapped around the tin cup. His eyes reminded Sue, a little uncomfortably, of Clare's expression as she lay on the pillow. Father looked exalted. He had always known that violence lurked beneath the world's order and quiet. He had been watching for it, braced against it, for twenty years. Could he help welcoming it when it finally arrived?

As the fires began to die down, the big old timbers snapping and falling, there began to be cool spaces between them. A breeze came up briefly, and all the faces grew anxious and then relaxed again. The eastern sky became rosy, and the first rays of the sun caught the rising smoke.

It was the first moment when you could really see that the barns were not there. Even more than their smoking, glowing heaps, what impressed Sue was the smooth slope of the big hayfield. All her life the barn had blocked view of that slope. Now she could see the top, just touched with gold.

Men were gathering pails and pumps, reluctantly getting ready to go home. It seemed wrong and incomplete to have them leave, but they had stock to feed.

Then the Campbells' handsome new express wagon came around the corner, Minnie driving and Aunt Emma beside her on the seat. With them came an aroma that brought tears to Sue's eyes and tears coursing down Mother's smudged face. Pies! Doughnuts! Real coffee, dark and mellow, and hot biscuits, and on both Minnie's and Aunt Emma's faces the warm floury look of people who have worked hard in the kitchen. The sun leaped above the horizon, and high in the scorched maple tree the rooster crowed.

23

After breakfast everyone left but Minnie, who'd been loaned by Aunt Emma to help get the house in order. Neighbors carrying their cups inside had made the kitchen even filthier than before. Still, Mother wanted Sue to go to bed.

"I can't," Sue said. "I'll set fast if I stop moving."

Mother stared at her, a wide-eyed stare that was more than exhausted. Mother was shaken to the core. When Father or the neighbors weren't around, she just stared at something no one else could see.

"Why don't you take Clare some tea and a doughnut?" Sue suggested.

"Oh," Mother said. "Oh, that's a good idea."

When she left the room, there was quiet in the kitchen, just the brisk stroke of the broom, the light chink of china plates as Sue stacked them away.

Then Minnie burst out, "I could *slap* Clare!"

Sue began folding the towels and tablecloths. Even in panic Mother had packed the good china carefully.

"You're not even mad, are you?" Minnie asked. "You all just *accept* this!"

Sue turned to look at Minnie. The air between them seemed full of tiny, shifting particles. "I . . ." Well, how could she answer Minnie? Of course they accepted this. It had happened. They all had made it happen, among them, and they must undo it or live with it. Being angry seemed somehow childish.

"None of my sisters would *dream* of a thing like this!" Minnie said, but her words had less force. She was studying Sue's face, as if trying to understand something. Sue felt a sudden sense of dread. When Minnie did understand, would they still be friends?

"No," she said. "Your family isn't like ours."

"You're right," Minnie said, sounding thoughtful and detached. "It isn't."

Sometime during the endless morning Reverend Stevens called.

"I have been admiring those old structures for forty years," he said as he came into the kitchen with Father. "They are a loss." He shook his head.

"Yes," Father said. His voice was hoarse and husky.

"It is like losing our parents all over again, to lose the work of their hands," Stevens said.

Sue leaned against the pantry wall, folding the damp dish towel and listening.

"Ah, well," Stevens said. "You and Henry will build a new barn, I suppose, and a hundred years from now that will be a revered old building. What is less easily mended is the hurt to this community. It will be like last winter, I'm afraid, everyone suspecting someone, ugly rumors flying—"

"Someone *did* do it," Mother said, in her new, faraway-sounding voice.

Reverend Stevens sighed. "Yes. Someone did." He took the chair Father drew out for him and sat musing. "It's very

129

sad. We have had so little crime in this valley. Not enough charity, not enough giving, but hardly any *active* evil. I confess I had taken some pride in that."

The kettle boiled. Minnie went to make tea, and Reverend Stevens looked up. "Minnie! Well, you couldn't have better help. And . . . yes, there's our Susan." His eyes warmed on her as she came out of the pantry. "I was told you had ridden out. I thought it must be one of the rumors that an event like this generates."

"No." It was all she could think to say.

"You managed to catch a horse and ride, with all that going on. . . . Which one? That black Morgan?"

"Not for sale at any price!" Father said.

"I should think not, David," Stevens said, but wistfully. "I've long admired him. Very like the colt that overturned my buggy one day many years ago, when I was driving a young lady out. You've heard me tell this, of course. She landed 'where the cow her kindly cushion laid,' and she didn't think enough of my horse jockeying to take the plunge and marry me. But the colt turned out very well, as I recall."

For a moment he seemed to gaze back fondly though the years. Then his eyes focused on Sue again. "Well, I'm delighted. You'll take my advice, I hope, and not let yourself overwork?"

"She won't be allowed," Mother said.

Sue kept her gaze on her folded hands, red and wrinkled from scrubbing. Mother's words sounded staunch, but Sue was already feeling the weight of her reliance, familiar, even welcome.

"And where is Clare? I saw Ed and Henry outdoors, but—"

"Clare is in bed," Mother said in a carefully neutral voice. She hesitated, then went on. "The excitement was too much for her."

"Oh?" Stevens looked from Mother's face to Sue's.

The fire had brought half the town down the long farm road to scrutinize their family life. "Sue Gorham got up from her sickbed, and Clare laid down in it!" She could hear the exact intonation of the words as the news rippled through the households of Westminster West. And the speculations: Was Sue ever *really* sick? Is Clare sick now? Questions that could not be satisfied except by the early death of one of them. Questions that would linger their whole lives long . . .

"Sue, you're falling asleep!" Mother's voice.

"I'll put her to bed, Mrs. Gorham." Minnie's strong arm around her, gently leading her upstairs, helping her unhook and slip out of her horse-reeking skirt and jersey. Then the nightgown, still in a crumpled heap before the closet door, smooth sheets, pillow beneath her head.

"Minnie?"

"Go to sleep." Suddenly Minnie's strong arms were around Sue, and Sue's cheek was pressed against Minnie's calico shoulder. "I love you, Susie!"

24

When Sue awoke, the light was coming in differently, and a feeling like dread weighed on her heart. Was something bad about to happen? She stretched her legs, the ache began, and she realized the bad thing had happened already.

She got up, pushing against pain in her hips, pain all down her legs, and put on a dress. Leaning hard on the banister, she went downstairs.

Minnie was gone, but a plate of her sand cookies lay on the table. Father sat there with his spectacles on, reading over his insurance policy. His early-morning look of exaltation was gone. He seemed older and very tired.

Henry had a bright red burn on his cheek and a defeated slump to his shoulders. Even Ed seemed less shining than usual: thoughtful, turned inward. Mother was briskly cooking them a meal—impossible to tell, in this mixed-up day, what meal it was—and speaking in a sensible, matter-of-fact voice.

"That's just a notion, David! Now I want you to think. Didn't you house a lot of Fred's sheep last winter, after their barn burned? And didn't you let them have some hay and even oats? It's just foolish, sinful pride not to let yourself be helped!"

Slowly Father nodded, as if the force of her argument had reached him through a haze.

Once again Mother was the center pole of the family tent. Her lined, pale, weary face showed discomfort with the role, Sue thought, but Mother must take it up again. She was needed.

"Hey there! How's our Paul Revere?" Ed pulled out a chair.

Sue sat down and groaned. "Sore!"

Father's bloodshot eyes focused on her. After a moment he said, "Bright was good for you?"

"He was *so* good!" Tears stung Sue's eyes. "He didn't even shy at Campbell's barn."

Father nodded gravely. "A good horse knows when you're counting on him."

"Is he all right?"

"Eating grass," Father said, and a faint smile lit his face, just for a moment. "Gave that Holden kid quite a time when the south wall fell."

"He only shied once—" Sue started to say. But Mother was making up a plate for Clare, and a stricken silence seemed to fall on the kitchen. Had it been this way when *she* had been in bed? She had not imagined the quality of her own absence until just this moment.

Over the meal the shape of the future began to come clear. The sheep and sow would winter at Campbell's. Father and the boys would throw up a lean-to and buy some hay for the cows and horses.

The plows and cultivators, the mowing machine and other farm tools had been burned. The whole year's work of shearing, haying, raising oats was lost. But they would not be bankrupt, and already Father and Henry were talking over the new barn they would build. Cut and haul timber this winter, that was agreed on, and they were heading toward strong differences about the barn's design when George Metcalf, the constable, and Daniel Wright, first selectman, arrived. A few minutes later Mr. Cutting, the state senator, drove into the yard.

"A bad business, David," Mr. Wright said, gripping Father's hand.

But they hadn't come to console. "I don't think it's an exaggeration to call this the greatest threat our town has ever faced," said Senator Cutting. "We must consider our course of action."

The men retired to the parlor. Sue helped wash dishes. Then she went outdoors.

The sun was setting behind bars of cloud, its rays golden across the ugly, smoking heap of the big barn. The barn was gone. It had burned, and she had seen it burning. But her eyes still expected it to be there. The hill beyond still came as a surprise.

Henry poked through the rubble with a half-burned board, looking for anything useful. Ed sat on the trampled lawn, sketching. "Once Henry gets his new barn built, we'll want to remember what this looks like," he said.

"I'll remember." The whole yard seemed strange, full of light that used to be blocked, too open. It made Sue feel uneasy. She went down to the barway and ducked through, out into the pasture where nothing had changed.

Bright watched her approach and then came to meet her. His coat was streaked with mud, and there was mud in his wavy mane, but his step was light and bouncy. He pressed his muzzle into Sue's palm and sighed.

"Bright," Sue said. Her heart swelled, smothering further words. She put an arm over Bright's shoulder and pressed her face against his warm neck. Together they had done the impossible. Gallop bareback all the way to the Campbells'? In the daylight, with nothing at stake, she could never do it.

This was what it must be like after battle, she thought. Your surviving friends must mean more to you than anything. And the men who'd risked you to gain their ends—the generals, President Lincoln, Father last night—must feel the way she felt about Bright: so moved, so proud, so humble.

Did Bright feel at all the way she did? Expanded beyond anything she'd ever expected of herself, sore and astonished, and able, ready for anything? Could a horse have feelings like that? Bright shook off a fly, dropped his head to graze again. If all his thoughts were innocent and simple, of food and company and comfort, then the events of last night were even more extraordinary. He had taken such care of her. Only once . . .

Once . . .

Sue found herself staring across the pasture, at the buckhorn thicket near the road. Right there. That was where he had shied.

Why? It had taken her this long to wonder, but now it seemed like the obvious question. In all that terrifying night, why did Bright shy just there?

Where was the firebug while everything was happening? Did he stay and watch? A chill spread down Sue's spine. So much had happened, there was so much to adjust to that she hadn't spared a thought for the person who had caused it. Had he been right there while she was riding past?

She loosened her fingers from Bright's mane and started toward the place.

The thicket was still green. The maple leaves were dropping fast, and the oaks turning color, but the slender, shrubby buckhorn kept its leaves a long time. They drooped and turned yellowish but did not fall.

In the dusk the thicket looked dark and deep enough to

135

hide someone. But it was empty now. Only a chickadee hopped from branch to branch, singing *dee-dee-dee* in its tiny voice. The grass was trampled, perhaps by the stock. Maybe Bright had shied at the thicket itself, a black bulk in the moonlight.

Too dark. I'll come back in the morning, Sue thought, and just then a mark seemed to take shape in the damp bare earth. A track.

The back of her neck prickled. Someone *had* been here. Bright must have smelled him, seen him. What if she'd fallen off? What if she'd landed in the road, right here in front of him? She wanted to run.

Instead she made herself bend and look more closely. There were many footprints, overlaid and blurred. Only one was clear: a big boot track with the mark of a patch on the heel.

Show someone! Quickly! Sue hobbled across the field, aching more with every step but loosening up, too. By the time she reached the barway she was actually running.

"Ed! Henry! I found a track!"

25

It was Henry who thought of using a bucket to cover the track and Henry who almost broke down when there wasn't a bucket to be found. It was obvious when a barn was gone. Only later did you discover that you were missing a hundred other things, from buckets to pitchforks to the bottle of horse liniment.

There were plenty of half-burned boards, though, and Henry carried one across the pasture, while Ed went to get Father and a lantern.

While they waited, Sue and Henry climbed over the stone wall and up onto the road. The light was even dimmer here, and many horses and wagons had passed over the surface. But the story of Bright's shy was still written plainly on the gravel, in a arc of deep-gouged tracks.

"How did you stay on?" Henry asked.

"I don't know." Sue felt again the way her leg had seemed to stretch, the right leg, which hurt the most now. She had almost fallen. She had felt empty air between her and Bright. "I'm glad I did," she said with a shiver.

"My God. Yes." Henry put his arm around her, something he hadn't done in years. Sue felt the tremble of his hand, smelled the sharp scent of his sweat. In some ways it was Henry she felt most sorry for. Henry had known his future so securely, and now it was changed overnight. She slid her arm around his waist and gave him a hug, and they turned to watch the lanterns coming across the field.

The lanterns cast a difficult light, and the men had to stand well back, in case there were other tracks that Sue hadn't seen. "Can't tell much tonight," George Metcalf said, and cast a worried look over his shoulder at the sky. The moon was rising, veiled in a soft haze.

"Don't think it'll rain," Father said, "but we'll put this over it." He had brought Mother's preserving kettle with him, and he placed it over the track. Metcalf put a heavy rock on top to hold the kettle down.

"Captain," Henry said over the fence, "here's proof he was here last night. Bright gave an almighty shy, right here. You know, we're damned lucky the son of a gun didn't end up killing Susie!"

The lanterns lifted and the hatbrims turned as everyone looked at Sue. Constable, senator, selectmen.

"Well, David," Daniel Wright said, "I'm in favor of putting up a reward, just as soon as we can hold a vote. This has to come to an end."

"I'll put up a few dollars myself," Senator Cutting said as they turned back toward the house. "It's our kind this fellow's after, you will have noticed. Those with something worth having."

"I'll stay this side of the hill tonight," George Metcalf decided, "if somebody'll loan me a bed. I'll look at that track again in the morning, and if you'll draw me a picture of it, young Ed, I'll take that down to Putney to show Jo Harris. Most of you do your cobblin' in Putney, don't you?"

"A lot of folks go to Otis Buxton," Senator Cutting said. "He does some cobbling work right there at the farm."

Father let them all through the barway, and they walked up the slope past the sheep barn. Coals still glowed within the heap of blackened timbers, and there was heat in the air. Ed and Henry would stay up all night, to make sure the wind didn't fan the coals to life.

"Stay here, George," Father suggested. "That'd be easiest."

"You don't need overnight company, David! Not with a sick girl in the house."

An embarrassed silence followed his words, hanging in the air like smoke. What a strange thing to say, Sue thought. As if Clare taking to her bed were the biggest thing that had happened.

But this was the fourth barn fire. You could almost get used to them. The odd behavior of the Gorham girls stood out, by contrast, as something that had never occurred before. People would wonder. People would talk. In the faint glow from the embers Father's face had a stricken, paralyzed look, and all the men looked down at their feet.

"I'll give you a bed, George," Senator Cutting said, and the group broke up in relief.

26

Friday's gray dawn found Sue awake, with the smell of smoke and burned wool in her nostrils and a deep, grinding ache in her right hip and leg. She had dreamed she was caught in a bear trap.

She sat up, and everything else hurt, too: her back and all down her ribs, her groin, her arms. She looked at herself under the covers. Had she turned black-and-blue overnight? No, her body was white, as always, with no visible sign of what it had been through.

The house woke up. Sue heard Father speak to Ed and Henry in the yard, the coffee grinder. Then, cutting through burned wool, the scent of frying bacon. Gradually, straightening one set of joints at a time, Sue stood up. Her feet didn't hurt, that was something! She belted on her dressing gown and hobbled down the stairs.

Mother was flying around getting breakfast. She gave Sue one keen look and placed her at the stove to mind the bacon. The heat penetrated to her bones, the bacon popped and sizzled, and Sue turned it carefully so it didn't crisp too much. "Where did we get bacon?" The last of their own had been used up in July.

"Mrs. Holden sent it," Mother said. "The things people

have sent—you'd think the *house* had burned, instead of the barn! Look at this!" She held up a jar. "If Eliza Coombs didn't send back the preserves I gave her this summer!"

Sue smiled, remembering butter, preserves, even mutton going from their own pantry to the Drislanes and Campbells and Uncle Mathew.

Father and the boys came in with the milk. Mother was making up a tray. Henry asked, "What's the matter with Clare now?"

"Headache," Mother said in a clipped voice, and Henry let out a sigh of disgust. Sue looked down to avoid catching anyone's eye. Henry's reaction was so simple he seemed like a child. But everyone else was silent, absorbed in private thought.

After breakfast Ed walked out with George Metcalf and sketched the track. The constable rode away with the piece of paper in his pocket.

A telegraph came from the insurance company, and Harlow's sawmill sent over a load of boards. "Pay me when you get darned good and ready," Henry Harlow told Father. He offered the loan of his son and of Herb Phillips, who was working for him at the moment. Between them they could knock up a shed in a couple of days.

"Herb Phillips," Henry muttered. "You don't think—"

"Herb's a good man," Father said. "Don't let this poison your mind toward your neighbors, son."

But none of them could help suspecting someone, and each neighbor stopping by during the day had a list. Alonzo Codding. Charlie West. Herb Phillips. Johnny Coombs. Young men who didn't have much, who might be resentful of those who did, each carrying a chip on his shoulder where someone in town was concerned.

"Wait," Father said to every suspicion. "Maybe George will have some news."

Meanwhile, moving slowly, Sue swept, and dusted, and wiped off the soot that had settled on everything in the house. If only she had been let alone to do that, she could have been perfectly happy. It was such a pleasure to be useful, to handle the broom, to touch all the family possessions after her long absence. Just to walk from room to room, glance out the windows at the grazing animals and the surprising heaps of smoking ash.

But every visitor wanted to see her and exclaim. She was like someone in a novel, a pale invalid raised from her bed by galvanizing danger. People seemed to set her miracle cure against the threat everyone felt, as if it balanced things out. Every marveling word struck a tender place inside Sue.

Was there a glimmer of suspicion on some faces, an inkling that this dramatic story wasn't really plausible? Sue looked hard for it, but overwhelmingly people seemed to feel only wonder and admiration.

The person Sue dreaded most was Aunt Mary Braley, and of course she came, walking into the kitchen with a basket on her arm and a bright expression on her face. She embraced Mother without a word and pushed the basket into her hands.

Then she turned to Sue, and a smile broke over her face. "It *is* true! I didn't dass believe it when I heard!" She folded Sue into a warm hug and then stood back, looking at her.

Sue forced herself to meet the old woman's eyes. She could feel the warm blush creeping up her face.

"There!" Aunt Mary said after a minute, giving Sue's

hands a squeeze. "You're where you belong to be, and that matters more than how you got there.

"You'll be thinkin' it's easy for the old woman to be cheerful about other people's troubles," she went on, turning toward Mother, "but I've had very comfortable news of Laura this mornin' and I'd be smilin' if 'twas my own barn. Now I know you don't need that mincemeat, but put it down cellar to please me!" She took up a rag as she spoke and went to rubbing the pewter plates as if in her own house. "Did you get your dried apples put away before this happened, Janey? That was all I could think about when I heard, and I stayed up past ten o'clock last night gettin' mine off the kitchen ceilin' and into a box."

"I got most of them, and the hogs got the rest."

"I tucked a few in your basket, just in case," Aunt Mary said. "And how's Clare? 'Bout as well as could be expected?"

Mother didn't answer for a moment. Then she said, "Yes, Aunt Mary, she's about as well as could be expected."

Just at suppertime George Metcalf returned. His shoulders slumped wearily, and his eyes were so sober that Sue knew he'd found something. He waited to tell until a place had been set for him at the table, a plate filled, and he'd taken a first appreciative bite. Then he sighed and met Father's eyes.

"Johnny Coombs. Buxton patched that boot for him a couple of months ago."

Father closed his eyes.

The constable said, "I went down to Jo Harris's, just in case, but Otis was pretty sure."

"I don't see it," Father said. "Everyone that's lost a barn

143

was a friend of Tolman's. What could Johnny have against his father's friends?"

"Did he have any reason to leave a track behind that bush?" George Metcalf asked.

"Well . . ." Father paused, and when he went on, his words came more slowly. "He came to look at pigs a few days before the fire. Said he might buy one—"

"And went all through the barns, didn't he?" Henry snapped.

"You don't need to go *through* a barn to know how to burn it."

"Why would he go behind a bush," Henry asked, "if all he came for was to look at a hog?"

"Son, sometimes a man does need to step behind a bush," Father said with the barest suggestion of a wink.

Metcalf looked around the table. "I'd rather this didn't get around if you don't mind. Buxton'll keep it to himself— because the truth is, one track and a horse shying isn't real evidence. I can think of ten explanations—"

"Name one!" Henry said.

George Metcalf looked steadily at him, not speaking.

"Then it's not proof?" Father asked almost hopefully.

"Not all by itself. We'll just have to keep our eyes open."

"Let's hope nobody loses a barn in the meantime," Henry growled.

27

On Sunday Sue stayed home with Clare. Sitting was still painful. She could never have made the two-mile trip to church, even with a cushion.

The house seemed quiet when the wagon was gone. The beans bubbled in their pot; the kettle hummed; the bright sun shone in across the geraniums on the windowsill and gleamed off the plates and glasses, all set on the table for dinner.

No sound came from the back bedroom. Sue hobbled up the stairs, one slow step at a time. This is how I'll walk when I'm a fat old lady, she thought.

The red book still lay in the back corner of her closet. She picked it up and stood weighing it on her palm. Really, Father's privacy would be best assured if she burned it. She should take it straight downstairs and put it in the range.

But Father could have done that himself, back when the words in the diary were raw. He had hidden the book, not destroyed it. What if he wanted it someday? What would he think if it were gone? Quietly she let down the attic ladder, and very slowly she climbed it.

In the attic she paused in the beam of light from the window and opened the red book at random. It fell open where it had stood open most often, the last written page. "What do you think I am?"

The words seemed to stagger across the page, expressing Father's bewilderment. What happened next? That question kept Father in Westminster West, got him married, brought them all into the world, but what was the answer?

There is no answer.

Sue sat on the rounded top of the trunk. There is no answer. What Father thought of Mother was one wrong thing— or if not wrong, then incomplete. What Mother had thought of herself was also incomplete. The night of the fire, when she'd seen what she'd made of Clare, she had understood that. You could never truly know someone else; Sue had long suspected that. Now it seemed that you couldn't quite know yourself, either. The heart had its own hidden motives.

Then what do you do? How do you live? Sue looked down at the trunk. When she'd last been up here, the only thing she'd wanted was to leave. But she knew so little about Westminster West, even now. Going out to the wider world would mean starting all over again. She had to go deeper here first.

And what about Clare? *She* had seen the wider world. Like Father, she'd come back full of damaging ideas. Like Father, might she be awakened? Was there some way?

Sue had barely seen Clare since the night of the fire. Mother carried the trays and did the sickroom chores, and it was from Mother that Sue had picked up a feeling of defeat, a sense that Clare would stay in bed, that this was the shape of the years to come. But Mother could be mistaken.

The dent and scratch on the book's leather cover showed Sue how to wedge it beneath the rafter so it looked as if it had never been moved. She got herself down the ladder, shook out her skirts, and went to Clare's room.

Clare lay propped on the pillows. Her hair was done up prettily in a Grecian knot, and she was reading. The back bedroom was very quiet. Not even the purr of the teakettle reached here, or the tinkle of a sheep bell.

"Clare," Sue said. Her heart knocked hard on the wall of her chest. Clare looked up. "Clare, how do you feel?"

"I'm all right," Clare said, on a faint note of surprise.

"Clare . . ." She must be very careful; she must not make Clare angry. "Clare, what—what happened Thursday night? Did you come outside? Did something hurt you?"

Clare's face slowly reddened. She looked stubbornly at the pages of her book. Keep quiet, Sue told herself. Wait.

"I . . . no. I didn't go out."

Wait.

"I felt . . . terribly faint," Clare said.

Sue closed her lips against a passionate surge of protest. Faintness was unchallengeable. Especially by her.

Clare said, "I'm not like you, Susie!" Her voice was quicker, sharper. "Everybody keeps saying, 'Sue can do anything.' Well, *I* can't! *I'm* no heroine!"

Tell her, Sue thought. I was well for nearly a month. I could have come down, but I knew what you'd do. And I was right. I was right.

She couldn't say it. A barrier in her throat seemed to prevent the words from coming. Clare was looking at her with perfect sureness in her wide blue eyes. Clare knew exactly what she was, what Sue was. . . .

"Clare." She had to push her voice out, and it would not say what she should say. "Clare, there are other ways. You don't have to stay in Westminster West just because the Campbells aren't going to Boston."

Clare lifted her brows in that new, plaintive way she'd picked up in the mountains. "Sue, you're sounding foolish, and it makes my head ache."

147

"Clare, *don't!*" Sue's voice sounded loud in the still room. "Don't *do* this!"

"*Do* this? *Do* this? What do you mean, Susie? Do you think I'm *faking?*" There was more color in Clare's face than Sue had seen in weeks. "You said that once before, you know. I wonder what put it in your head!"

Tell her. It was the one thing that might shock Clare out of her course.

But then Clare would always know. She would always have that power, and the wrong Sue had done would never again be hidden.

Seeing Sue silenced, Clare went on. "I don't see that I'm to be blamed for having a more delicate system than yours! It's not my fault I'm not like you!"

You are like me, Sue thought, gazing at Clare's pretty, firm-jawed face on the pillow. You're so much more like me than I ever dreamed!

The clock struck the half hour, one soft, heavy, resonant chime. It seemed to strike within Sue's heart, too, as solid and physical as a blow. She turned away from Clare without another word.

There was no barn to hide in. For the first time Sue truly felt the loss as she stood on the front step with tears running down her cheeks.

She sank onto the step and pressed her face against her knees, forcing her sobs to be silent. The hard stone hurt her aching bones, and that felt right.

The tears didn't last long. Sue wiped her eyes and blew her nose. She could smell the beans drying out, but a great weariness kept her sitting on the steps for several minutes longer.

She had put away the diary feeling so much older, so full of understanding. She would go to Clare, she would ask a magic question, and everything would be all right. How silly and childish that seemed now! How foolish she had been!

Yet if it had worked, it *would* have been wise. If Clare had been different. If she had been different. If she had dared tell Clare the truth.

But even that might not have changed anything. Clare had imagined she could be part of Julia Campbell's world. Absurd, but it wouldn't seem that way to Clare. She had been treated like a princess for years, invited into the Campbell household twice. Her hopes must have seemed reasonable. If Mother had guessed, she might have nipped them in the bud. But no one had guessed.

Now, thwarted, Clare fell back on her only other acceptable plan of life. Perhaps she did have headaches. Perhaps she was even faint. The mind could trick the body, Sue knew that. But whatever trickery was going on, it would last a long time. If Clare couldn't leave Westminster West on her own terms, she wouldn't leave at all.

And I won't leave either, Sue thought. Clare had trapped them both.

That realization seemed to suspend all thought. Sue just sat, seeing the smooth yellow-green hill stretch up toward the sky, sunlight gleam off the black, shining char of the burned timbers. A blue jay perched there, head cocked. Now it drifted with swift, miraculous lightness to the ashes to peck at a cinder.

28

THE NEXT SUNDAY Sue went to church.

It might have been the same trip she'd made in June, except that Clare's seat, and Mother's, were empty. Sue hadn't quite realized how the whole family was never together anymore.

"World look good to you, Susie?" Ed asked, and she jumped.

"Yes," she said, beginning to take it in.

The trees were bare now, the whole landscape turned yellow and brown and stark. Frost glittered in the shadowed places. Houses that had been hidden behind the leaves for six months were plainly visible. High on Perry Hill the gray Coombs house looked like an abandoned wasps' nest. Below it the new Campbell hay barn stood out fresh and yellow.

Deacon Buxton passed, and the Millers came up behind. Bright and Lucky would not let them by, but Father paid little attention to the game. Sue twisted on her seat and looked back at the lively family in the wagon, and baby Bertha waved.

When they drove into the churchyard, it was plain that something had happened. Angry faces, frightened faces, a cluster of people around George Harlow and his wife, touching and consoling them.

"I *told* you!" Henry said. "I said we shouldn't wait!"

"Henry," Father said, "shh."

Ed helped Sue down from the wagon, and she went over to Minnie and her family, five freckled little sisters in descending sizes, like a set of organ pipes. "What happened?"

"Two of their barns burned yesterday, ten o'clock in the morning." Minnie looked sober, standing beside her anxious father. "He's getting bolder. It's the first time he's burned something in broad daylight."

All through the sermon everyone's eyes were on the person in the next pew forward; everyone's ears seemed to strain to hear a whisper from the person behind, the person beside.

After the service the young men clustered in the churchyard, in knots that seemed to shiver and vibrate with strain. Their eyes had a challenging, dangerous brightness, and they watched one another as they spoke. Sue heard talk of dogs, of slow matches, and detectives.

The suspects were as much in the thick of it as anyone. Alonzo Codding, Charlie West, Herb Phillips, young men with no families, no connections, hardly anything of their own. They had always been well liked, but really, who knew anything about them? They had no parents here to stand behind them, no known histories and genealogies to turn over and examine, as everyone else's history had been examined.

But there was no evidence. Who could accuse them without doing a great injustice? They joined the groups of men, speculating along with everyone else. Johnny Coombs was absolutely the center of the knot of young men, eyes aglow, more important than he'd ever been in his life. Perhaps Henry had said nothing, but suspicion settled on Johnny anyway. The Harlow boys watched everyone, hot and hungry, waiting for a slip.

151

Minnie came up and put her arm around Sue's shoulders. "How is Clare?" she whispered.

"The same." Sue couldn't take her eyes off the boys. Even Ed wore that warlike, wolfish look.

Minnie said, "They love this."

Love this? Sue looked around at the pale, grim faces, the sober and watchful eyes. Yes. Somehow, deep down, everyone *did* love it. In danger they drew together, sensed one another, depended on one another. If only they knew who the enemy was . . . But we can't know, Sue thought. Each person here was in some way a stranger.

Yet each was also known. Each counted. Each changed things for everyone else, even Johnny Coombs beside his rotten old buggy, and Minnie's five little sisters with the braids down their backs. If you could look down from above, you would see each person the center of the group, spreading a circle of influence that overlapped and underlay the other circles. Even the headstones on the hill spread influence, and the horses in the sheds, the church building itself, and the big maples that shaded it.

"Minnie . . ."

Minnie glanced at her. "Yes?"

"Minnie, aren't you glad you live here?"

Minnie laughed aloud, making several people glance at her. "I'm glad *you* live here, Sue Gorham! And as I stand here looking 'em over, I'm kind of thankful for those Harlow boys, too. What do you think?"

29

THE JAR OF PRESERVES that had gone to Mrs. Coombs and come back again was bundled into a basket for Mrs. Harlow, along with a package of Mother's special mixed mint tea and a sympathetic note.

"It wasn't their *house* that burned," Sue said, teasing, and Mother gave her a look.

But a week later it was the house—in broad daylight, eleven-thirty in the morning. The Harlows were able to save many of their possessions, including most of the furniture, but the house was completely destroyed. The two remaining barns were burned as well, so the hay and oats that had been saved before, and rejoiced over, were gone.

"This is our fault," Henry said when Charles Hall had come and gone with the news. "We have to *do* something!"

"There's nothing legal or decent we can do," Father said.

"We can watch him—"

"We've sent for a detective," Father said. "If you've been reading the papers, Henry, if you've paid attention to what's going on down south, you know how ugly things can get when people take the law in their own hands."

"It's pretty ugly when people lose their homes—"

"Henry," Father said, very sadly, and Henry shut his mouth hard and kept it shut.

On Sunday Father asked him to stay home with Clare. As soon as the wagon was out of sight, Sue thought Henry probably got out the rifle.

There was a stranger at church, a large man in a brown suit, with a beefy, red face and a city hat. Father said he was Jarvis, the Boston detective, and he watched everyone with hard, impersonal eyes. It was impossible to be natural. People lingered in the churchyard for only a short while before heading home.

Monday was the first washday Sue could handle by herself. Last week she'd still been stiff, and Minnie had come.

It would have been nice to have Minnie here now. But Sue enjoyed the feeling of returned strength and the knowledge that no one else was needed. The smell of starch and blueing, hot metal and wet wool, gentle slosh and heavy pull of lifting soaked garments: she felt that her eyes, her ears, all her senses were opened to it. If she were Ed, she would record washday with her pencil, catching the beautiful line and fall of fabric. But so much else would be left out: the way the lye soap stung and the water slopped on the floor, a word with Mother, and a few minutes later, another.

Besides, was there any need to record washday? It would go on, week by week, forever. The need was simply to be here with open eyes and ears.

Tuesday morning they were ironing when a buggy pulled into the yard. The sound of hammers stopped, they heard excited voices, and suddenly Ed was at the door, a rush of cold air sweeping in with him.

154

"They've arrested Johnny Coombs! He's out here in the buggy!"

Mother set her flatiron on the stovetop. "Sue!" she said, and with a start Sue lifted her iron off the petticoat frill. The cloth smelled hot, but there was no scorch. She followed Mother to the door.

A black buggy stood in the yard, a lean brown trotter between the shafts. A heavy man with a mustache held the reins, and on the seat beside him sat Johnny Coombs. He wore manacles on his wrists and a look of complacency, even pride on his face. His long, arching dark eyes glanced around the farmyard at the great heaps of ash, charred timbers, and debris. He seemed to be smiling. But he said nothing.

"Jarvis and Reverend Stevens got him off by himself," the fat man told Father, "and talked things over with him, showed him the picture of the track. And he said he might as well plead guilty. Takin' him over to jail in B.F. now."

Mother's hand reached back to her apron strings. "Has anyone gone to his mother?"

"Yes, Mrs. Gorham," the fat man said. "I'm Lovell, ma'am, deputy sheriff from Bellows Falls. Yes, Reverend Stevens is there right now."

Sue watched Johnny's face. She could see no change when his mother was mentioned—no embarrassment, no shame. Johnny Coombs looked like a man well satisfied to be just where he was, as if he had achieved something important.

Across the buggy from her Sue could read the bafflement on Father's face. Not even Henry seemed triumphant. Johnny Coombs in chains seemed a trivial thing beside the heap of char and ash and the empty space in the air where the barn had been.

"I'll be gettin' along," Lovell said. "Just thought you'd want to know, and since I was passin' . . ." He seemed disappointed, as if he'd expected a bigger reaction from them. "There'll be a hearing tomorrow. Someone'll let you know." He set the horse in motion.

"Do you suppose maybe he *didn't* do it?" Ed asked as they stood watching the buggy turn around. "Is he fool enough to say he did just to be the center of attention?"

Father shook his head slowly, mutely. The buggy rolled away up the road, past the buckhorn thicket where the track had been long since rained away, and the scars of Bright's shy wiped out by passing wagons. The buggy top was up, so Sue couldn't see if Johnny looked toward his hiding place.

The buggy tilted to one side under the deputy's weight. The brown horse's hooves flashed and clopped between the wheels. A little lurch as the horse leaned into the collar to take the hill. Then they were around the corner and lost from sight.

"David," Mother said, "I've got to go up and see if I can help her. At least let her know we don't blame *her* for what's happened."

"Yes," Father said, vaguely, as if he felt far away from everything. "Yes, that's right. Henry, harness a horse for your mother."

Mother hurried into the house, taking off her apron as she went. "Sue, will you get me my coat? I wonder if I should take her a little something. . . ."

Sue hugged herself tight. She was shivering deep inside, but she couldn't help laughing. "I shouldn't bother. Remember those poor preserves?"

Mother turned blankly. "What? Oh, I suppose they got burned with the Harlows' house, didn't they? No, I won't take anything. She won't have the heart to eat. Let the fire go, Sue, and we'll finish when I get back. You might tell your sister—" With her coat half on, she was already out the door.

Sue went slowly back through the house to Clare's room. Johnny Coombs . . . Of course it was Johnny Coombs. Like Clare's going to bed, Johnny's arrest had that odd clarity of something foreordained. Yes, you thought, when such a thing occurred, but it was never clear enough beforehand.

"They've arrested Johnny Coombs," she said from the bedroom doorway.

Clare looked up from the little book of poems she was reading. Her eyes widened, and she pressed her hand against the base of her throat in the way that had made Minnie so angry. The ruffles at her wrist, the lace at the yoke of her white nightgown made the gesture even more graceful and effective. "Then it's all over?"

"Probably," Sue answered. In spite of everything, she found that she was smiling. How well Clare did it, after all! She herself had never been so good at it, had never made her sickroom a sanctuary and a realm: the soft afghan in the rocking chair, the dainty shade on the lamp, the letters and little gifts from friends, the small, prettily bound books, and the delicate embroidery within the round, dark hoop.

And young women did fall ill, and who could discern the line between illness and intention? Who really knew anything about another person? There was a different version of this story, Clare's version, and Sue didn't know what it was. Perhaps there were many excellent reasons.

"Can I bring you anything, Clary?"

Clare's eyes widened involuntarily, and she flushed. "No.

No, thank you." She hesitated. "Come sit on the bed a minute and I'll rub your arm. I know how ironing makes you ache."

Sue's arm did ache. She had been enjoying the feeling actually. That was strength coming back. But she sat on the bed, and Clare massaged her forearm, and she felt the knowing strength of Clare's fingers. Tears stung her eyes for no reason that she could fathom.

30

On Wednesday Justice Lane held court in the crowded chapel. Sue didn't go. Someone had to stay home with Clare, and the prospect of seeing Johnny in chains, of hearing his slow mind twisted and exposed to the light by Justice Lane's examination, was not pleasant.

As it turned out, she missed nothing. Johnny waived examination and refused counsel. His course was all marked out, he said. "I might as well plead guilty, for you'll prove it against me, although I am innocent."

But he had admitted knowing about slow matches, when questioned by Reverend Stevens, and that, combined with the track and other circumstances, left little doubt. Lacking bail of three thousand dollars, Johnny was taken to the county jail in Newfane, to await the convening of the grand jury in March. The *Brattleboro Phoenix* noted, "His bearing was that of a proud self-consciousness, as though he was the chief actor on an important occasion."

Father was prosecuting. Because of the strong evidence provided by the track, Johnny would be charged first with the Gorham fires. Sue could only guess what Father thought about that. He was silent and sighed often, perhaps remembering Johnny's father. Everyone had loved Tolman Coombs. There was something so sweet about him, so quiet. He always seemed to be resting from pain, or resting between pain, in a kind of stunned passivity. Now his only son was Westminster West's enemy.

Mrs. Coombs was heard to be feeble, dazed, and shocked, but few people saw her. Even Mother was gently turned away after the first day, when a niece came up from Dummerston to take over. The shame was too great. She did not know how to face her neighbors. A week to the day after Johnny was arrested, the niece walked down the hill to Campbell's to say that Mrs. Coombs was dead.

The gray house was left empty, the livestock fed twice a day by a Campbell hired man. A week after Mrs. Coombs's death the stock and feed were auctioned off.

Father didn't want to go. He didn't say so, but Sue could sense his discomfort. He was willing to send Johnny Coombs to state prison, but it seemed a different matter to profit from the sale of his inheritance.

"It's one-thirty," Mother reminded him, looking up from the ironing. Father sat at the table, unmoving. "It's oats and hay, David, and only half a mile away. Wouldn't it be silly not to go?"

At that Father smiled wryly and reached for his hat. "Jane, you always put me right. Where would I be without you?"

"I can't imagine!" Mother said. Did they all think of the west? Sue wondered, licking her finger and touching it lightly to the bottom of her iron to test its heat. Did they all go on to reflect, for just a moment, on the war and a question asked at a front gate: "What do you think I am?" And did each of them assume that this thought was entirely private? She pressed the heavy iron across a breadth of dark calico skirt and watched the color seem to brighten as the wrinkles smoothed out.

* * *

Father bought enough of Johnny Coombs's hay and oats to take him well into the winter. He and the boys brought home a load of hay and stacked it by the new shed. Leaving Ed to finish topping the stack so it would shed water, Father and Henry went back with the big team for another load.

When Ed was finished, the others hadn't yet returned. He came in for the milk pails, and Sue went out with him to help do the chores.

The sun was setting. Sue looked toward the place in midair where the barn roof would have caught the last red rays. Now the sunlight passed through, invisible. Ed sat on a stool with his head buried in the cow's flank. Milk hissed into the pail.

From the sack in the new shed, Sue measured out oats for the horses. Bright and Lucky jostled at the fence, and the young hogs dodged and squealed beneath their hooves. Sue dumped the oats into the wooden trough and watched the horses lay back their ears to menace each other, bite the hogs' backs.

"What was the auction like?" she asked, pausing to lean on the cow's back and breathe in her sweet scent.

Ed shrugged. "Short. Cold." He stripped out the last milk and stood up. "Like butchering, you know? When you forget the critter was ever alive and start cutting up the pieces? All the work poor Johnny did all summer—"

"He burned *your* work," Sue said.

"Yes, well, we all come out ahead somehow. Everybody gets a big new barn out of it, and Johnny's sitting in jail with not a soul left on earth who cares for him." Ed's mouth closed in a thin, bitter line, and he stood for a moment looking up the frozen farm road.

Sue followed him in her mind, left at the main road and downhill to the corner of Westminster West road. There Ed

161

was turning south, away from the village, toward Putney and Brattleboro and the wide world.

"Why do you think Johnny did it?" she asked, mainly to keep Ed here a moment longer.

Ed turned impatiently. "It made him important! He's somebody now! I keep thinking if we'd tried harder to like him, none of it would have happened."

No, Sue thought. For none of it to happen, the whole fabric of the world would have to be unraveled, such a long way back. To keep Johnny from going to the camp, from catching the fever that damaged his mind, there would have had to be no war, no slavery, and what could have prevented that?

If there'd been no war, if Father's mind had never been shaken, if Mother had not needed to become the pole to which he and all of them clung, what else would be different? Who would they be, she and Clare, Ed, and Henry?

A hog squealed under Bright's teeth. Father and Henry were coming down the road now, wagon wheels loud in the frozen ruts. The oven door banged. Sue took the milk pails from Ed, their cold fingers brushing, and went inside.

A wave of heat struck her. She stopped in her tracks. The door slammed behind her, and Mother turned from the stove. "Sue, will you—" She stopped. They stared at each other. Sue felt her heart swell and ache with a sorrow she couldn't name.

"You look like a wild thing," Mother said quietly. She came and took the milk pails, bringing with her a cloud of warmth and cooking smells. "Go outside while there's still light. Go on, I can get supper without you."

"*Thank* you!" Sue said, bringing a funny little smile to

Mother's face. Then she was out the door and almost running up the long slope of the big hill.

The last time she'd been here was to pick wild strawberries. Now the fields were yellow-green, the ground was frozen, and the grass gave and crunched beneath her feet.

At the top of the hill Sue swept the folds of her skirt beneath her and sat. The last sunlight turned the eastern ridges a soft mauve. She watched until it was gone and the sky had turned lavender with coming night, the bare trees standing in black silhouette.

She leaned back on her elbows. The field stretched down away from her, as if she were lying on an enormous over-turned bowl that held her up near the sky. She chewed a short stem of grass, sweetened by frost, and watched the first star come out.

"Thank you," she whispered. Thank you for the field and the sky and the branches of trees. Thank you for this world. Thank you because no one was hurt in any of the fires, and because Bright came out of the dark pasture in answer to her call.

Thank you—did she dare think this?

Yes. Only here, close to the sky, and alone, she could be thankful that she had seen Mother collapse at the kitchen table, that she'd seen Father fight the fire. Here she could be thankful for her illness, glad that she'd done such wrong, dared to lie and fake. It had done no real harm to anyone else, and in the end it had done her good.

And here, thank you, thank you, to Johnny Coombs. Thank you because she was out here on this beautiful evening with the first star just appearing, because he had gotten her down the stairs in a way there was no going back from.

How hard it would have been to get herself down, admit to being better, and come back to everyday things.

Now it was done. Johnny had lost everything, Clare lay in bed, and the barns were gone. Much harm done. But good had resulted, too, great good, and she was thankful.

She sat up again. She could see the ridges that defined Westminster West, darkly shouldering the sky. Between them the land lay in velvet blackness. Vast fields might be concealed there, or deep abysses, wilderness—or simply a narrow valley, a few farms, and a little village where lamps were being lit and everyone was sitting down to supper.

Cold seeped up from the frosty ground and into Sue's bones. She stood and shook out her skirt and walked down the dark hill toward the lights.

AFTERWORD

How much of this story is true?

Most of it. A young man named Johnny Coombs did burn several buildings in Westminster West, Vermont, during 1883 and 1884, causing a considerable stir in the community. The fires and Johnny's arrest and trial are all documented in local newspapers. The burning of the District One schoolhouse is a rumor of long standing, but I have not found any historical account of it.

Johnny's father, Tolman Coombs, was a Civil War veteran and died in 1883. His mother died a week to the day after her only son's arrest for arson. The auction of the Coombs livestock and fodder is mentioned in the *Brattleboro Phoenix* of the following week.

The story of the Gorham sisters is found in *Vignettes of Westminster, Vermont,* an unpublished collection of anecdotes written by their contemporaries, Frank Miller and his sister, Bertha Miller Collins, and left to the Westminster Historical Society. The Gorham story is presented in *Vignettes* as a curiosity, and Bertha Miller Collins concludes, "No one ever knew what physical or mental aberration caused one girl to leave her bed in a calamity and the other to retire from activity on the same night."

There is no other documentation of Clare and Sue Gorham's story. This is my own interpretation.

165

Students of Westminster West history will notice a degree of poetic license. The Gorhams are all younger in this story than they were in 1884. Other people's ages also have been altered to suit the needs of fiction.

I have found no record that David C. Gorham served during the Civil War, although a flag decorates his grave.

The road currently known as Beebe Road I have called Perry Hill Road. I have no idea what it was called at the time, but as the Perrys had lived there for many years, the name at least seems possible.

Much information exists about Westminster West in the early 1880s. *The Windham County Gazetteer and Business Directory* was published in 1884. It lists each householder and business in every town in the county, telling on which roads the families lived, what their occupations were, how many acres they owned, and in some cases what breeds of livestock they raised.

The Fortieth Anniversary Address of Reverend Alfred Stevens was delivered in 1883 and published in Abby Hemenway's *Vermont Historical Gazetteer*. It gives a forty-year perspective on the town. The section on Westminster West's history in Hemenway's *Gazetteer* was also written by Stevens.

Many of the anecdotes in this story are drawn from *Vignettes of Westminster, Vermont*, compiled and edited by Rachel V. Duffalo, with help from my parents, Bob and Pat Haas. It is offered for sale through the Westminster Historical Society.

I have lived all my life in Westminster West. I grew up in the Hall house. The house next door, now owned by my sister, is the one owned in 1884 by Patrick Drislane, and beside it is the barn Drislane built to replace the one burned by Johnny Coombs. The farm on which Clare and Sue Gorham lived is less than half a mile down the road. It is now owned by David and Cindy Major and is operated as a sheep dairy, making award-winning cheese.

Johnny Coombs pleaded guilty to setting the Gorham barns afire. After serving his sentence he was rearrested on the prison steps and charged with setting the Campbell fires. He served another sentence and was again rearrested, to be charged with the Drislane fire. Charges were dropped when he agreed to leave Vermont after serving a total of eleven years for his crimes. He departed for a Massachussetts shoe-making town, where he planned to practice the trade he had learned in prison.

Ed Gorham went to music school in Boston. He became a singer and a singing teacher there, and also painted landscapes and portraits. After he retired, he came home to Westminster West and helped record the town's history. His poems, photographs, and paintings enrich Elizabeth Minard Simonds's *History of Westminster.*

Henry Gorham became one of the most successful farmers in Westminster West, living all his life on the family farm.

Clare Gorham, according to *Vignettes,* "never again regained the strength to be up and around the house until the very last days of her life." She was "a lovely, quaint character . . . gay, chatty, and rather irresponsible" (*Vignettes*). After his retirement Ed urged Clare to get back on her feet and resume a nearly normal life. She did begin to attend social gatherings when he was present, and she took over much of the housework. This was probably after Sue's death in 1921. Clare lived until 1936.

Sue Gorham continued to live on the family farm and is mentioned in *History of Westminster* as having inherited a silver loving cup from Delyra Goodhue. The cup was given to Delyra by Homer before they were married, and the bequest suggests a close friendship between Sue and the older woman.

A postcard mailed to a friend in Washington, D.C., by Clare Gorham, dated December 23, 1910, gives insight into the household at that time. Father had died in 1907, but Mother "is having a comfortable winter, works or reads all the time. Susie has had trouble all summer with her throat and in Oct. was very bad—she was not able to do anything for awhile. Can only whisper now and has to dose for it all the time. Coughs very bad at times. We expect Ed home Sunday for a weeks vacation. . . . We have not had many callers this winter . . . are alone most of the time."

But on a brighter note: "Sue was surprised to receive a card from you away down there for her birthday—she had 261 cards, a great surprise for her but she enjoyed it."

Maybe it was a surprise, but the two hundred and sixty-one birthday cards delivered to the farm at the end of the road show that Sue Gorham had a true gift for friendship.